MATTERS
OF THE
HEART

MATTERS
OF THE
HEART

•

Terry Zahniser
McDermid

AVALON BOOKS
NEW YORK

PRINTED IN THE UNITED STATES OF AMERICA
ON ACID-FREE PAPER
BY HADDON CRAFTSMEN, BLOOMSBURG, PENNSYLVANIA

To my own family, for their constant love and support,
and to my Royal Heights friends—Thank you!

Chapter One

" "W here is she?"

Christine Hunter carefully pushed back her chair and stood up, turning a calm face toward the man hurtling toward the hospital admittance counter. "May I help you?"

He leaned over the narrow ledge separating them, his hands gripping the polished wood. "They called and said my sister was here. How bad is she?"

Christine picked up a clipboard. "When did she come in?"

"I don't know." He ran a hand through dark windblown hair and took a deep breath, stepping back from the counter. "A half an hour ago at the most. I was out of my truck and it took a few minutes for them to find me."

She glanced up and narrowed her eyes as she recognized him. "Jake Reynolds?"

"Yeah." A question entered his deep brown eyes. "Do I know you?"

"Probably not." She skimmed a finger down the few

1

names listed on the admittance sheet. "I was a freshman the year you took us to State."

"Boy, that was a long time ago." He leaned one denim clad elbow on the counter. "You've grown up since then."

"A bit." She nodded toward her clipboard. "I don't see anybody named Reynolds on the list. Are you sure they brought your sister to the hospital?"

"Yeah. But her name wouldn't be Reynolds. It's Anna Belton."

Christine relaxed. It was easier to deal with distraught relatives when the news was positive. "She's okay. I saw her when she came in. She may need a few stitches but that's all. The doctor was waiting for somebody to give us permission."

"I can do that."

"Then let me take you back."

The clipboard tucked under her arm, she came around the counter and headed for a pair of heavy white doors. His work boots clicked on the tiled floor, the sound muffled when they reached the carpet.

Pausing next to the desk in front of the door, she smiled at the older woman sitting behind it. "Ethel, would you watch admittance until Emily comes back from her break?"

"Sure, Christine." She nodded at the man next to her. "Hi, Jake."

He gave the woman a grin that Christine remembered from her high school days. It had made her knees wobbly then and it still did. Watching Ethel's eyes light up, she figured most women were susceptible. "I thought you were going to retire."

"And do what?" she countered. "Stay home and watch soap operas? I see better plots here."

Jake chuckled and followed Christine toward the emergency room entrance. When he reached over her shoulder and pushed the doors open, she inhaled a whiff of the outdoors before the antiseptic odors of the hospital brushed it away. The doors opened with a soft swoosh, the rubber casing at the bottom sweeping across the tiled floor, and she stepped away from him, reminding herself she wasn't a teenager anymore.

The emergency room area was quiet and only two sets of curtains were closed off. "She's right here," Christine said, holding back the first pair of curtains.

Jake walked under the opening and stopped. "Gee, Anna, what did you do to yourself?"

Christine peeked around his arm, surprised at his comment. The little girl sitting in the middle of the bed looked grimy and dirty, but her forehead didn't look that bad. The blood had been washed off by the school nurse and a butterfly strip had been taped over the jagged cut to keep it from bleeding. Christine was pretty sure she would need at least four stitches, but other than that, she could see no reason for Jake to be so upset.

She stepped forward and wrapped a protective arm around the girl's narrow shoulders. Anna stiffened but didn't pull away. "She's okay, Jake," Christine said with a warning in her eyes.

He shrugged. "Maybe her forehead is. But her hair." He brushed at the uneven bangs covering her forehead. "What did you do, try to cut your own hair?"

Amazed, Christine watched Anna's brown eyes fill with tears. "The teacher said they were getting in my eyes too much. I thought . . . I just . . ." She hiccuped and stopped with a big sniff.

Christine bent down until she was eye level with Anna. "You cut your forehead cutting your bangs?"

Anna sniffed again and nodded. "So I could see better. I mean, she kept griping at me about my hair being in my eyes and I got tired of it so I just took my scissors and cut them off. But I couldn't see and I cut my forehead."

Jake leaned against the wall at the end of her bed, one boot crossed over the other and his hands jammed into his jeans pockets. "Why didn't you just pull them back with that barrette thing I got you?"

" 'Cause I lost it!" Anna snapped.

Christine bit back a grin at the sibling exchange and then swallowed it when she saw Jake's glare. She straightened up and tugged down her blue–flowered smock, smoothing it over the contrasting slacks. "I'll see if the doctor's free yet," she murmured.

The curtain opened before she took a step. "Hello, there." Dr. Sanders walked into the room and paused next to Anna's bed. "I understand you need some stitches, young lady."

The little girl sent Christine a frightened look. "It won't hurt that much," she assured her.

"Really?" Jake's drawl was quiet, but she glared at him, afraid Anna could hear.

"Not after the first little jolt," she said. She's only a little girl, she thought. Was he so mad he was deliberately trying to upset her?

"Here." She handed him the clipboard and tapped the attached pencil. "Fill out these forms while you're standing there."

"Now?"

She gave him what she hoped passed for a sweet smile. "So we know what we can do. Unless you'd rather have your mother fill it out when she gets here."

"She's dead," he said baldly.

Silence filled the air between them. She hadn't meant to be rude and she wished she could call back the words. He might have been one of the local stars during his high school years, but she had little knowledge of his life since then.

The star running back during his years in high school, Jake had set records that were still posted on the gymnasium wall. After graduation, he had disappeared for a few years. Christine had heard he had returned to Durant, starting up a construction business while she was still in nursing school. He had quickly built himself a reputation as a businessman that was as sturdy as the homes he built for people.

Not that Christine had much reason to see him. They existed in separate worlds, her friends younger than his and not inclined to frequent the same spots.

She glanced at the little girl on the bed. Dr. Sanders' quiet voice and gentle manner were easing her worry, and she answered his questions with a piping voice. She can't be more than seven or eight, Christine thought, wondering about the girl's father. Jake's dad, another football legend in the area, had died before his son started high school. The local newspaper had followed the team's move toward the state championship, often noting how sad it was that his father didn't see him take the team all the way. Jake's last run his senior year had led to their school's win.

She shook off the memories when Dr. Sanders quietly asked her to prepare the instruments he would need. When Anna's brows drew together, Christine gave her a big smile. "It's okay, honey." She smoothed the stringy brown hair behind little ears and eased Anna flat on the bed. "Dr. Sanders is really good."

"Will you stay with me?" Anna whispered.

Christine glanced at Jake. He was still lounging against the wall, but she thought he looked more like a panther ready to pounce than someone relaxed. "Sure, honey. And your brother's here, too."

Anna ignored the last sentence. "Will you hold my hand?"

"Don't you want your brother to hold it?"

"I'd rather have you." Anna's dark eyes locked on Christine's face.

She spared Jake one more glance. The family resemblance was subtle, but she could see it in their eyes, the way they speared you with a single look. He shrugged, the motion tightening the jacket around his broad shoulders. Christine quickly turned her attention back to the little girl, determined to keep her mind on professional thoughts— and not on the rugged man in front of her. "I'm here."

Carefully removing the small bandage, she smoothed a white cloth over Anna's face, positioning the opening over her cut. She picked up the little hand. "What grade are you in, Anna?"

"Second." The little girl's voice was muffled, but she didn't sound scared.

"Second grade. I bet you're reading now, aren't you? A friend of mine teaches kindergarten at your school." She handed the doctor the cream that would numb the area. "In fact, she's married to Dr. Sanders."

The doctor scooted his stool closer to Anna's side. "Now, Anna, I want you to take nice, easy breaths and just relax."

As the doctor stitched the wound closed, Christine chatted about the weather, the new puppy she was trying to train, and several other mindless topics she hoped would distract Anna her from the doctor's movements. Jake shifted his feet with every tug of the doctor's needle, but she didn't dare drag her attention away from the little girl. She hoped he didn't faint. They could only deal with one patient at a time.

"Done." Dr. Sanders stood up and carefully pulled the cloth off Anna's face.

They both stood there a moment, watching the steady rise and fall of the little chest and the flutter of her lashes against her cheek. "You talked her to sleep," Jake said, humor deepening his voice.

Dr. Sanders laughed, peeling off his gloves. "Saves on anesthesia."

Christine bristled at their teasing. "At least she wasn't scared."

"No, she was very brave." The doctor dropped his gloves into the trash can and held out a hand to Jake. "Good to see you, Jake. Sorry it had to be this way."

"Well, that's the way it is with kids."

Greg laughed. "Yeah, they do keep you hopping."

Christine busied herself with cleaning the area around the bed, feeling left out of their conversation. Single, without even a favorite niece or nephew, she only knew about children from her married friends. And she suspected they didn't always give her a very reliable picture.

Not that I don't like kids, she told herself as she dropped the disposable instruments into the trash can and slid the others into a pile for washing later. *Mandy's new daughter is fun. And I do a pretty good job when I talk to the classes at school.*

She rolled up the paper cloth that been spread over Anna's face and dropped it into the trash can, turning in time to hear Jake ask Greg about his search for property. She waited for Greg's answer, knowing he and Mandy wanted to build a house that would be their own. With Jake's reputation, she could understand why they would have talked to him about it.

Greg shook his head. "No. Amanda has her heart set on something close to town that gives the feel of country. She doesn't want Jessie isolated from her friends and yet she wants the open space of the outdoors. Funny, since just last year, she thought the city was the perfect place to live."

"Women." Jake shifted away from the wall and stepped toward his sleeping sister. "What about Anna?"

"She'll be fine." The doctor pushed open the curtain. "Miss Hunter will go over the directions for caring for the stitches and you can bring her back in four to five days to have them removed."

The curtain snapped closed behind him. Christine straightened from her tasks, suddenly realizing how small the space was. Leaning against the counter and then against the wall, Jake hadn't seemed that tall. Now that he was standing next to her, she had to tip her head back to meet his eyes.

"I have a sheet here for the care of stitches," she began in a stilted tone.

"She doesn't have to stay home or anything, does she?"

"No. She probably should go home for the rest of the day, but she can go to school tomorrow, if that's what you mean."

"Yeah." He ran his hand through his hair. Gold and red highlights flickered in the bright hospital lights. "A neighbor lady watches her sometimes after school but I don't think she'd be up to all day."

"What about when Anna's sick?"

"So far," he knocked on the wooden cupboard above the sink, "she hasn't been sick. Until now."

He slanted a glance at the sleeping child and Christine saw his expression soften. "Should we wake her up?" he asked, turning his gaze on Christine.

She shook her head. "She's probably tired from the trauma. She's had a lot happen in the last little bit. It's okay if she sleeps. It's not like this was a head injury. She just cut through her skin."

"Cutting her own hair. Gee." He crossed one hand over his chest and used the other to rub his chin. "I never know what she's going to do next. I didn't realize how hard one little girl could be."

"Are you her sole guardian?" She told herself she only wanted to know for Anna's sake, but she was relieved when he nodded his head.

"Yeah. Our mutual grandparents died before she was born. She stayed with her other grandparents right after the accident, and I think they considered contesting the will. But after having Anna all summer, they decided that maybe Mom knew best after all." His grin was rueful.

Poor little thing, Christine thought, glancing at the little girl curled up on the bed, the stitches dark against her pale skin. To lose your parents at such a young age and then be bumped around like that.

"I'm sorry about your mom," she said softly. Her own parents were still a very vital part of her life.

"Thanks." He rubbed a hand over his chin again and then stuck his hands in his back pockets. "She and Anna's dad were in a car crash in May. Nobody knows for sure what happened, but they think Frank had a heart attack and drove off the road."

"Oh, that's terrible."

"Listen, I was wondering if you could help me."

She turned her attention back to him and away from the orphan in front of her. Two orphans, she realized. "What?"

"I left a crew of men at a job site waiting for me and I need about two hours before I can get away. Do you know anyone who could watch Anna for me until I get back?"

"You're not going to take her home?" She couldn't believe he was going to abandon his sister after her trauma. Maybe she didn't know a lot about children, but she knew it wasn't right to leave a little girl after a visit to the hospital, even if it wasn't major surgery. Her sympathy shifted away from him and landed on his sister.

"I can't." He glanced at the clock over the sink. "I need to drive out there and give them some instructions before I can go back home."

"What about phoning them?"

"Won't work. They don't have a phone in the middle of the lot, and even if they did, I can't explain what they need to do without showing them."

"She'll be upset if she wakes up and you're not here."

He shook his head. "Probably not. She barely knows me. We may be related, but we haven't seen each other more than half a dozen times, and most of those were before she was two."

Christine frowned. Her life hadn't been sheltered, but his family relationships were certainly different than most she had seen.

"I get off in thirty minutes . . ." she began.

"Great." He folded the instructions she had given him and tucked them into his back pocket before pulling out a set of keys. Twisting them around, he detached two and handed them to her. "These are for the front door. The address is on that form I filled out."

She stared at the keys and then at him. "Whose address?"

"Mine. I don't know what's in the refrigerator, but make yourself at home. Anna's usually starving by the time she gets out of school."

"You want me to watch Anna?"

"Hey, thanks." He glanced at his watch again and edged toward the curtain. "Listen, I don't want to be rude, but if I leave those guys by themselves very long . . ."

"I can't watch Anna."

That stopped him. "Why not? You said you get off in thirty minutes. She'll probably sleep that long."

"Yes, but . . ."

"You don't have other plans, do you?" he interrupted.

"I might!" she sputtered.

He gave her his famous grin. She gritted her teeth. *I will not let him charm me into doing this.*

"I wouldn't ask for this if I wasn't in a bind," he said, backing away from the bed. "I really appreciate it." He pushed the curtain back on its rings. The sound rattled down her spine. "I'll be back in two hours."

She stared at the empty space, wondering if she had imagined that he had ever been there. At a rustling behind her, she sighed and turned around, pasting a smile on her face. It wasn't Anna's fault her brother was an arrogant tyrant. She'd give him his two hours and then she'd let him know what she thought of his high-handed ways.

Chapter Two

The two hours stretched into three and then four. Christine rummaged in his refrigerator and found some eggs and cheese that didn't look outdated. While Anna sat at the kitchen table, Christine whipped up an omelet and made toast with bread that was almost ready for the trash bin. After the simple supper, she tucked Anna into bed, read her a story, and clicked off the light.

She was wiping down the counter when she heard whistling and a key in the back door. Carefully dropping the wet paper towel into the trash, she turned around and waited for Jake's apology.

He didn't give her one. Instead, he glanced around the sparkling kitchen and let out a long whistle. "Pays to have a nurse for a babysitter." He plopped down on a kitchen chair and began unlacing his boots.

"I didn't do it for you," Christine muttered. "Anna shouldn't live in a place like this."

He paused, one hand poised above his laces. "What?"

"This place is a mess, Jake. No food, dirt on every avail-

12

able space. When was the last time you mopped the kitchen floor?''

He rubbed his hand over his cheek, scratching at the growth of beard that had appeared since she saw him at the hospital. ''I don't know. We don't eat here much. Anna has breakfast and lunch at school, and we usually just grab a bite somewhere in town.''

Christine snorted. ''Which gives her a healthy choice. The restaurants in town come in two categories, Jake. Fast food and sit-down classy. I don't imagine you favor the classy ones.''

He dropped his boot on the floor. Christine grimaced as dust and mud landed on the newly mopped floor. ''How do you know what I like?''

She gestured toward the work boots tossed haphazardly on the floor. ''Last I heard, Albany's required at least a tie. I don't think work boots would fit their style.''

He spread his stockinged feet toward the counter, effectively blocking her from leaving the room without stepping over his long legs. His blue jeans molded his lean legs, reminding her just why he had been able to move so fast on the football field.

He leaned back in his chair, his hands laced behind his head. ''Any other criticisms?''

She started to shake her head and then nodded. ''As a matter of fact, I do have a few other concerns.''

''Why am I not surprised?'' he muttered.

''Listen, I didn't ask to take care of Anna. You bulldozed me into it.''

''Bulldozed.'' He grinned, surprising her with how quickly his expression could change. He hadn't been the most handsome boy in school, but he had always been considered attractive. Looking at his twinkling eyes and the big grin on his face, she knew why the girls had whispered about him in the corridors.

He yawned and twisted his head back and forth several times. Lines of fatigue spread from his eyes. "Those crazy guys were ready to start knocking down trees when I got to the site. I tell you, I have to watch them every minute. The owners told me at least a dozen times they wanted me to leave the oak trees. If even one had been knocked down . . ."

"I'm sure this is very interesting," she interrupted with what she hoped was enough sarcasm, "but we were talking about Anna and the way you're caring for her."

"We weren't talking about it, you were," he supplied gently.

She stepped away from the counter, her hands on her hips. "I could report you, you know. As a nurse, I'm required by the state to report any instances of neglect. . . ."

He was on his feet in an instant, his hands gripping her arms just above the elbows. "Neglect? I was ready to humor you about the lack of groceries, but neglect? Can you honestly say I'm neglecting my sister?"

She tried to back away from the anger in his eyes, but he had her in an ironclad hold. "I didn't mean it that way. It's just that . . ."

He released her and swung toward the sink, opening a cupboard, pulling out a glass, and filling it with water. She rubbed her arms and watched the back of his head as he gulped down the water. "I think you should go now," he said when he was finished.

"Jake, I know this has to be hard on you, a kid coming into your life like this."

He didn't turn around. "She's my sister. What was I

going to do, turn her over to the state? Oh, right, that was your idea.''

She flinched. ''Jake, I'm sure you care about her. I saw you at the hospital, remember? But caring isn't enough. She doesn't have any dolls, hardly any books. Her room looks like she's visiting and she's been here for more than a month.''

''So she likes being outside more than playing with dolls or being cooped inside reading. Doesn't mean she's neglected.''

Christine took a risk and stepped forward, placing her hand on his arm. He didn't shrug her off, but he didn't turn around. ''I don't think she is, not really. It's just that . . .'' she hesitated, wondering how to broach the topic without offending him. ''She needs to feel like this is really her home.''

''Do you take this much interest in all your patients?''

That stung, and she backed away from him. ''You're right, I'm overstepping my bounds.'' She scooped up her purse and her jacket. ''She should sleep through the night. You can bring her back to the emergency room or go to Dr. Sanders' office when it's time to take out the stitches. Call if you need anything.''

She was almost to the back door when his voice reached her. ''Listen, how much do I owe you for the babysitting?''

She froze and then turned around slowly. He was holding his wallet open in one hand, several bills in the other. ''I did not do this for money,'' she said carefully. ''In fact, you couldn't pay me enough to do this again.''

''Christine?''

Her shoulders drooped at the quiet little voice from the hallway. ''Anna, I thought you were asleep.''

Anna rubbed sleepy eyes. Her stitches and jagged bangs

gave her a waifish look that struck at the core of Christine's heart. "I heard shouting." She yawned and looked at her brother. "Mommy and Daddy used to fight all the time, too."

Jake picked up his sister and cuddled her in his arms. "We weren't fighting. We just didn't realize how loud we were talking. Come on, I'll take you back to bed."

"Will you tell me a story?"

He pursed his lips and she put both hands on either side of his face. "One?" she asked earnestly.

"A short one." He tossed Christine a grin over his shoulder. She shook her head at him, acknowledging that Anna did not look neglected.

Anna yawned again and rested her head against Jake's shoulder. "Will you come, Christine?"

"No, I have to go home." She didn't want to think about how much she liked the sight of Jake's big hands softly caressing the little girl's hair. He looked natural, as if he had been caring for her since she was a baby.

"Good night. Thank you for playing with me." She gave another big yawn and blinked her eyes several times. "I liked the supper," she said sleepily. "Jake never cooks."

Christine grinned and this time, Jake acknowledged the hit with a quirk of dark eyebrows. "Maybe we'll go grocery shopping tomorrow," he said.

Her lips still curved upward, she let herself out of the house. Evening was coming earlier now that summer had made way for autumn, and the sky had darkened. A few stars sparkled in the dusky sky and the moon was slipping over the treetops. She stretched her shoulders and climbed into her car.

Excited yapping greeted her when she opened the door of her tiny house. The real estate ad had described it as a "bungalow," which she had quickly learned meant it was small and cramped. But she liked the sloping roof, the arched doorway between the kitchen and living room areas, and the twelve acres of undeveloped land behind it. With no access to a road, the property wouldn't be developed easily, giving her the advantages of both the country and the city.

Just what Mandy wants, she thought, unbuttoning her smock and dropping it into the hamper. Not that her tiny house would provide much room for a growing family. For one person, eager to get away from a large, boisterous family, it was just perfect.

She neatly stacked her shoes in the closet and added her slacks to the laundry pile before draping a thick robe around her shoulders. Armed and ready, she made her way to the small pantry off the kitchen. A baby gate separated the two rooms and a puppy jumped and scrabbled at the plastic lattice work.

"Hey, you, stop that." She bent down and scooped him up, scratching him under the neck. His tongue slopped kisses over her cheeks until she held him away from her.

"So, did you scare off any burglars today?" She smoothed her hand over his back as he whimpered and arched toward her.

When she set him on the floor, he dashed into the living room, sniffing around the bottom of the furniture, poking his nose into the potted plant that grew in front of the window and then dashing down the narrow hallway that led to the bedroom. She heard his frustrated yowl when he discovered her door was closed and wasn't surprised when he came trotting back in while she was washing her hands.

"Four shoes are enough for any puppy," she stated, taking out a package of dog food and pouring it into his bowl.

"That black pair was my favorite." He bent his head and chomped at his food without any indication of remorse.

She opened the cupboard above him and pulled out ingredients, stacking them on the counter, wondering if she was a little crazy. She didn't know why she was making cookies. The evening hadn't ended the way she had envisioned. She had meant to be calm and collected when she told Jake she didn't like being used that way. Two hours indeed! Thank goodness tomorrow was her day off. What if she had needed to wash her uniform, run errands? Had he even considered her plans?

The first panful of cookies ready for the oven, she carefully stepped around the puppy. His initial hunger sated, he lay on the floor, his paws crossed in front of him and his head practically in the dish as he nibbled on a few hard squares. She nuzzled his neck with her bare foot and he sighed.

The phone rang and she reached for it without moving from her place at the counter. One advantage of a small place was that nothing was too far away.

"Hello."

"Christine?"

She jerked to attention, her elbow hitting the edge of the counter. Tears spurted to her eyes as she rubbed the aching joint while jostling the phone.

"Jake? Is Anna okay?"

"Yeah, she just went back to sleep. Hey, listen, I wanted to thank you for staying with her so long."

"It's okay." She didn't want an apology. Her anger was easier to hold on to if she could remember that he had abused her kindness.

The timer dinged and she opened the oven door, being careful not to trip over the puppy. He had finished his food and was sitting up, his head cocked as he watched her move around the kitchen, the phone tucked between her shoulder and ear as she listened to Jake.

"Anyway, I hope I didn't mess up any plans of yours."

She liked the way his voice sounded over the phone, low and deep, with just a hint of gravel under each word. In her own kitchen, with the smell of fresh baked cookies wafting around the room, she could dismiss her earlier feelings as nothing more than a desire to be home. Not that it wouldn't hurt to remind Jake he needed to consider others. "No, it was fine. Of course, Rocky was a little upset because his dinner was late."

"Rocky?"

She glanced at the puppy, who had lifted his head at her use of his name. "Yeah. He gets a little growly when he doesn't get fed on time."

"Well, I . . ." She could hear Jake swallow, which made her grin. Serves him right for being so arrogant. "Tell him I'm sorry."

"Oh, he's okay now. Just took a little cuddling."

"I see."

The line was quiet so long, she thought he had hung up. "Well, um, I guess I'll tell you good night," he said finally. "And thanks again."

"You're welcome. Good night."

She hung up the phone and smiled at her companion. "Maybe that'll teach him not to treat people like they don't have lives of their own. How did he know I didn't have a husband and a houseful of children waiting for me to come home?"

She slept in the next morning and then ran her uniform and other laundry through the pint-sized washer and dryer that sat on top of each other in the pantry. Rocky raced around her feet, jumping and nipping at the clothes each time she moved a load. "Get down!" she said for the thirtieth time and nudged him away with her foot.

The doorbell rang as she was folding her towels on the living room couch and watching a game show. "Don't you touch those," she told Rocky as she went to the door.

He gave her a limpid look from his place in front of the television set and dropped his head back on his paws, chewing on the rawhide she had given him. She didn't trust him and kept her eye on the laundry as she pulled the door open.

Her mother stood on the postage-stamp front porch. Several inches shorter than Christine, Catherine Hunter had the same red hair and green eyes as her daughter. "I was hoping you'd be home. You wouldn't want to grab a bite with me, would you?"

Out of the corner of her eye, Christine saw Rocky tug a towel off the couch. "Rocky, give that back!"

She lunged toward him. He made it under the kitchen table before she wrestled away the towel, one end soggy from his mouth. She secured him behind his gate, dropped the dirty towel on top of the washer and went back into the living room, ignoring his whimpered pleas.

"Don't say anything," she said to her mother.

Her mother lifted both hands. "I wasn't going to say a word. I think it's marvelous he only got away with one towel. You're making progress."

Christine folded the last of the towels and scooped them into her arms. "It's the gate, actually. My laundry loads have been cut down tremendously since I put it up."

She slid the towels into the linen closet and joined her

mother on the couch, clicking off the television as she sat down. "Where did you have in mind?"

"Maybe Albany's." Her mother glanced at Christine's sweatsuit. "Of course, since it's your day off, you may not want to dress up. It's just that your dad's out of town and I need to do something besides rattle around in that empty house by myself."

"Albany's is fine. Dressing up and wearing my uniform are two different things." She reached over the side of the couch and picked up the newspaper, handing a section to her mother. "That movie we wanted to see is in town. Maybe it has an early show."

"That would be fun. Your dad said he'd take me, but I know he wouldn't enjoy it. 'Too mushy,' he'd say. Why I married such an unromantic man, I don't know."

Christine laughed. "Because he swept you off your feet." She stood up. "I'll change while you check on the movie times. I have a few errands to run but they won't take long."

They ate a leisurely lunch, leaving just as the business crowd was arriving. Christine and her mother greeted several people they knew, making their way slowly toward the front door. Saying goodbye to an elderly couple she had known for years, Christine was surprised to hear her name called in a deep, gravelly voice.

She lifted her head and met the dark brown eyes of Jake. "Hello, Jake."

"Hi. I didn't expect to see you here." He glanced at the emerald green suit she was wearing. "Day off?"

She nodded. "I'm not chained to the hospital."

"Jake, our table's ready." The blonde at his side paused, her brows pulled together as she looked at Christine. "Christine Hunter, right?"

Christine nodded, wondering if all the women she knew were at least a foot shorter than her. She didn't mind her height, especially when she was faced with a man as tall as Jake Reynolds. But once in a while, she couldn't stop from wondering what it would be like to be small and delicate.

Like Marilyn Peters. The local real estate agent gave the impression of a fairy princess, with her blonde hair, blue eyes, wearing the misty grey suits she favored. Not that she was delicate when it came to real estate deals. She had been the agent for the sellers of Christine's house and her hold had been as tenacious as Rocky's on a towel.

"Business lunch?" Christine asked sweetly, noting Jake's suit. A far cry from the clothes he had been wearing the day before. The crisp white shirt emphasized the sheen of his sunbronzed skin, while the grey suit darkened the color of his eyes.

"Oh, I always like to mix business with pleasure," Marilyn said, wrapping her hand possessively around Jake's arm.

One corner of Jake's mouth lifted. "You? Here on business or meeting Rocky?"

Her mother joined them at that moment. "Rocky? Here?" A tiny chuckle erupted from her lips. "Now that would be a sight."

Christine grabbed her mother's arm before she could say any more in front of Jake and Marilyn. "It was nice seeing you again," she said, including both of them in her comment. "Enjoy your lunch."

She didn't give her mother a chance to say a word, propelling them both out the door at a breakneck speed. Not until they were safely on the sidewalk did her steps slow.

"What was that all about?" Catherine brushed a hand

over her hair, smoothing down several curls that had been loosened in the mad dash.

"What?" Christine kept her face averted from her mother.

"That race out of the restaurant. I thought maybe you heard the fire alarm."

"Sorry, I forgot you needed a slower pace for your little legs."

"Christine Hunter! What a rude thing to say to your mother! I've been keeping up with your dad all these years without a single complaint."

Christine unlocked the car door for her mom and turned, certain her expression would give away nothing. "That's because he never wanted to hurt your feelings."

"Remember, young lady, I'm still your mother."

Christine dropped a kiss on the top of her mother's head. "I know. That's why I don't mind walking at such a slow pace."

Her mother was shaking her head when Christine slipped into her own seat. "Somehow, I failed," she said in a quiet voice.

Christine started the car, knowing what was coming next.

"I thought I could raise you to be a polite young woman, but your father and brothers conspired against me."

Christine grinned. Whenever she didn't fall into her mother's plans or showed she was an independent young woman, her mother tried guilt. "I didn't turn out that badly."

"No, but I did think I'd have a few grandchildren by now."

Christine slowed down for the one stoplight and glanced at the woman calmly sitting next to her. "What brought this on?"

"The fact that instead of having lunch with a nice man like Marilyn was, you're going out with your mother."

Her heart pounded and she turned her attention back to the road. That "nice man" had once had the power to make her bones turn to water, but she wasn't about to tell her mother that. Especially not with her in a matchmaking mode.

She decided to shift her mother away from the topic of Jake. "Mom, I'm the baby, remember? Why don't you get after the boys?"

"Because they don't listen to me."

"And you think I would?"

Her mother didn't answer right away. The light turned green and Christine headed toward the edge of town.

"Now I know who that was," her mother said suddenly.

"Who?" Christine kept her eyes focused on the road. The traffic was light, but the drivers were making frequent stops at the businesses she was passing.

"The man with Marilyn. I thought he looked familiar, but I couldn't place him right away. It was Jake Reynolds, the football player." She shifted in her seat until she was facing Christine. "Do you know him?"

Her mother was as stubborn as Rocky. "I met him at the hospital yesterday," she said carefully. "His sister had to have stitches."

"His sister? I didn't know he had a sister."

Christine nodded, braking as the aged Cadillac in front of her signaled for a turn. "She's about seven. Her parents died last spring and Jake is her guardian now."

"Oh, the poor little thing." Her mother folded her arms over her chest. "I'll have to make them some of my salmon chowder and take it over. It can't be easy for him raising a little girl by himself."

"He's doing okay," Christine said, ignoring the implied question. If her mother wanted to know if Jake Reynolds was available, she would have to do her own checking.

"Your father would love to talk to him. He and your brothers still talk about that last game of his. The only time we were state champions. Even his dad didn't get us that far."

"More to life than football."

"True, but it wouldn't hurt to be neighborly. I never could understand that mother of his, flitting from man to man after his dad died. But that's not Jake's fault. I'm glad he moved back to town. His houses are in demand."

"Not surprising, since we don't have that many local builders around here."

She couldn't stop the sharp note entering her voice and she winced, knowing her mother would hear it.

Her mother's reaction didn't surprise her. "Christine, I taught you better than to use that snippy tone about people. What has Jake Reynolds ever done to you?"

"Nothing." She wasn't about to mention watching his sister for him. With her mother's recent comment about grandchildren, she was not about to give her any fuel.

She turned into her driveway, feeling about five years old. "I just hope you don't talk about him that way to anyone else," her mother said, unbuckling her seat belt as the car rolled to a stop. She leaned over, kissing Christine's cheek. "Maybe you need a nap. You work so hard. If you think the movie would be too much . . ."

"I'm fine, Mom." Christine patted her mother's hand. "I'll meet you at the theater about 4:45. Thanks for lunch."

An hour later, the plate of cookies on the passenger seat mocked her as she drove back downtown, stopping first at the drycleaners, then the library and the electric company.

What would Mom say if she knew you were bringing cookies to an eligible bachelor? She'd probably start shopping for wedding dresses.

After settling a discrepancy in her electric bill, she drove the short distance to Jake's house and parked on the street in front of the single story structure. She had expected a larger, more ostentatious place based on the few examples of his buildings she had seen. The owner of a local trucking company lived in a five-bedroom home complete with two fireplaces and a swimming pool, compliments of Jake Reynolds and his building crew. Her insurance agent had just moved into a new house that boasted its own hot tub on a covered porch.

From her visit the night before, she knew the house in front of her was sturdy and functional. Anna's room had a built-in window seat and cupboards in the walk-in closet that erased the need for a dresser in the room. The kitchen might have been messy, but she couldn't fault the design, and the living room was spacious without sacrificing comfort.

A horn sounded behind her and she saw Jake wheel a black pickup into his driveway. Sighing, she opened the door and took out the plate of cookies.

"Hi, what are you doing here?" He wrapped his arms around two bags of groceries and kicked the cab door of the pickup shut.

She had hoped to leave the cookies on the back steps with a short note, never dreaming he'd be home in the middle of the day. "I brought you some cookies."

He glanced at the plate she held and headed down the drive toward the back door. She had no choice but to follow him. "A peace offering?" he asked.

"Why would I bring you a peace offering?" she sputtered.

"I don't know." He juggled the bags until he had both in one arm and used his free hand to unlock the door, holding it open so she could go in first. "Maybe because you made those accusations about me?"

She stopped in the middle of the kitchen floor. Stay calm, she admonished herself. "I just thought you'd like some cookies," she managed to say. "I usually bake something on my day off, and I thought you and Anna would enjoy them."

"Rocky didn't mind you bringing them over?" He shrugged out of his jacket and started putting fresh fruit in the refrigerator, cans of soup under the counter, cereal in the cupboards.

She took a deep breath and exhaled slowly. "You know, Rocky is my puppy."

"What?" He raised his head quickly and banged it on an open cupboard door. Biting back an oath, he rubbed his hand over the sore spot. "Rocky is a dog?"

She nodded, chewing on her lower lip. "He did growl when I came home late," she excused herself.

"Rocky is a dog," he repeated, leaning against the counter and crossing one ankle over the other. "Here I thought I'd gotten you in trouble with some tough named Rocky."

"You didn't know if someone was waiting for me at home," she said.

"Was someone?"

"No, but that isn't the point." She handed him a box of cereal, which he added to the growing collection in the cupboard. Was he planning to live on cereal?

"What is the point?"

"You took advantage of me, Jake. You asked me to watch Anna for a couple of hours and I ended up being here almost five. I fed her dinner, put her to bed, and then you didn't even apologize when you got in for not calling or for being so late."

"I apologized when I called you."

"Yes, well . . ." It still didn't absolve him from coming in so late, as if she didn't have a life of her own.

He paused, one hand on a cereal box. "Are you sure it was five hours?"

She nodded. "Five hours. It was almost eight-thirty when you got home."

"I am sorry." He rubbed a hand over his chin. "I mean, I knew it was getting late because it was getting dark but I didn't realize . . . . Listen, if you won't let me pay you, at least let me take you to dinner tonight."

A wave of pleasure washed over her at the thought of going to dinner with Jake Reynolds and then disappeared. "I can't. I promised my mom I'd go to the movies with her." *Not that Mom wouldn't willingly rattle around the house for days if she thought I had a date. But she's not going to know about this.* "My dad's out of town and she's a little lonely."

"How about tomorrow then?"

She mentally scanned her calendar. She had to work but she could be home by four o'clock. She could spend the time looking through her wardrobe, fixing her hair . . .

She forced herself to relax. He was taking her to dinner as a thank you. Nothing else.

A tiny glimmer of excitement wouldn't disappear. She could feel her pulse speed up. "Tomorrow would be fine.

Nothing fancy, though, right?'' She would keep her expectations low.

"Of course not." He grinned. "Anna hates getting dressed up as much as I do."

Chapter Three

She told herself she should have expected it. After all, he hadn't been able to find a babysitter when Anna cut her head. Why should she expect him to find a sitter so they could go out to dinner?

Not that it didn't hurt a little bit. He had taken Marilyn to lunch without the added attraction of a little girl. Why couldn't she have the same thing?

She frowned at her reflection in the mirror. Just once, she wished she didn't look like somebody's kid sister or the girl next door. Even tamed in a short cut, her red curls looked wild. They did shine from brushing and the green sweater brought out the color of her eyes, but the freckles on her nose and cheeks took away the look of sophistication she had been trying to achieve.

"Not that it matters," she muttered to an interested Rocky. He had been watching her for the last ten minutes, after discovering she had emptied the bathroom trash can before letting him into the room. "He won't notice my make-up. At least, we're going to some place that caters to kids, and Anna will enjoy herself."

She brushed one last coat of mascara over her lashes and clicked off the bathroom light. Rocky's nails clattered on the tiled floor before he safely made it to the carpeted hallway. "Sorry, bud, I forgot you were in there."

She tucked him into his space behind the gate and dropped several chew toys and a rawhide bone in front of him. "I'll be home before it's late," she informed him. "Anna has school tomorrow and I have an early shift."

The doorbell rang at six-thirty, and she opened it to find Anna and Jake on her doorstep. "Can I see your puppy?" Anna asked. "Jake says he growls if you don't feed him."

"He's male," she said with a sweet smile. "They can't go for long without food or they get cranky."

"At least we're not picky about our food," Jake said, following her across the living room. He ducked at the archway and then rubbed his hand over the curved opening.

"Nice work. This place has been around for a while." He knocked on the wall. "Sturdy."

Some of her tension and frustration melted away. So it wasn't a date. He was nice and Anna was a charmer. "Since the twenties. I think the original owner must have been from southern California and was trying to re-create that type of house here."

"You could be right. You don't see many in this style around here."

Anna was kneeling by the gate. She reached over the divider and had her arms bathed by Rocky's tongue. "Oh, look what he's doing," she giggled.

Christine bent down and pushed the inquisitive puppy away from Anna. "Be nice."

"He wasn't hurting me."

"No, but his tongue is full of germs. You'll have to take a bath after you're through with him, if you're not careful."

"She likes baths," Jake murmured. "She takes one the first Saturday of every month."

Christine gave him a puzzled look and then frowned at him. "Okay, I'm sorry, I'm sorry, I'm sorry. I was tired and frustrated that night and didn't mean half of what I said."

"Which half?"

She lifted her hands in surrender. "You win. You have now effectively made me crazy. You can mete out whatever punishment you want to."

He laughed and tucked his hands into the front pockets of his jeans. "Okay, I'm done. But you have to admit, you gave me lots of ammunition."

"I didn't. You gave it to yourself." She turned on the kitchen faucet and kept her finger under the water until it turned warm. "Let me help you wash up, Anna. I'm sure your brother must be getting hungry."

Anna patted the puppy's head. "I'll see you later." She glanced at Christine with a question in her eyes. "I can see him later, can't I?"

"Of course. You can visit anytime you want to." She rubbed Anna's arms with a soapy wash rag and then helped her rinse off.

"Does that go for Anna's brother?" Jake asked.

"I don't know." She unhooked a towel from the wall and dried Anna's narrow little arms. "It depends if you're good."

"Oh, I'm very good."

The breath caught in her throat and heat rushed into her cheeks. She swallowed and concentrated on drying Anna's arms. His tone hadn't changed but she was sure she had caught an underlying current in his words.

She carefully hung the towel on the rack and slowly turned around. The ceiling light glinted on the ends of his hair, turning them a rich mahogany. The tips of his lashes were flecked with gold and sparkled in the glow from the light. His dark blue shirt molded his broad shoulders and flat stomach, and the worn jeans accentuated his powerful legs.

"So, where are we going?" She kept her voice light, hoping he couldn't see how his comment had affected her. He might have brought his little sister along, but he was acting like this was an actual date.

Of course, it could just be habit. She'd seen how the girls followed him around when he was in high school. Her own group had been guilty of a few whispered conversations about him, complete with melting looks and deep sighs. No doubt he was used to women falling at his feet and expected the same reaction wherever he went.

"Pizza," Anna stated before Christine had any more time to think of the implications of dating a man like Jake Reynolds.

"They have a salad bar," Jake added, lifting his hands when Christine glared at him. "Sorry, I couldn't help it."

She picked up her jacket from the back of a kitchen chair. "Pizza's fine. In fact, it covers most of the main food groups."

"Food groups? You mean, like chips, burgers, and pop?"

Anna giggled. "No, she means dairy, meats, fruits and vegetables, and breads and cereals." She glanced at Christine with a proud look on her little face. "That's right, isn't it?"

Christine rubbed a hand over Anna's hair. She really needed a trim to even out those bangs. Maybe she could suggest Jake take her to a beauty shop. "You're exactly right, Anna. Maybe your brother needs to go back to school. Though he does seem to know the cereal group," she said, remembering the cupboardful she had seen yesterday.

"We like cereal," he said, holding the door open for the two of them and then waiting for Christine to lock it before following her down the flagstone path to his truck. "It's easy to fix and we don't buy those sweetened ones."

His black pickup was parked behind her small compact. He opened the passenger door and boosted Anna over the step and onto the wide seat. Christine grabbed the door handle and hauled herself in before he could touch her.

"Not bad," he said, waiting as she settled on the seat. " 'Course a country girl like you, you've probably been in a lot of pickups."

Before she could respond, he slammed the door shut and walked around the front of the truck. Anna leaned over and honked at him and he jumped, his arms going wide.

Christine shook her head at his antics. Even at his worst, he could make her chuckle. She knew he hadn't been surprised by the horn and imagined it was a ritual between them. She and her brothers used to flip the wipers on before their dad got in, and she could remember their insane giggles when he turned on the car and found them swishing across the window.

He climbed in the driver's side and started the engine. "Buckled?"

"Of course."

He leaned over Anna. "You'd be surprised how many

people don't buckle up. But then, you being a nurse, I can imagine you're cautious about a lot of things.''

He shifted the car into gear. She frowned out her window. What did he mean? Did he think she was boring?

She glared at him. ''Just because I buckle up and eat healthy food doesn't mean I'm . . .''

''Huh-huh-huh,'' he interrupted with a jerk of his head toward Anna.

Christine subsided in her seat, still seething. What was the matter with being sensible? It didn't mean she didn't enjoy a good dose of craziness every now and again. And so what if she was careful and neat about things? The world didn't need a lot of nuts running around doing crazy things.

She sighed and leaned her elbow against the door rest. She should have politely declined his invitation and cut their relationship off before it started. From the moment they met, they had been at cross purposes. Her life might be quiet, but it suited her.

''Everybody wanted to see my stitches,'' Anna announced in the growing stillness.

Christine welcomed the reminder that she wasn't alone with Jake. ''I bet they did. Did you tell them how brave you were?''

Anna nodded. ''Whitney got stitches in her chin last year but she only got three. I have the most in my class.''

''How exciting,'' Jake drawled dryly.

''Stitches are exciting,'' Christine said to his profile. ''Especially when you're in the second grade.''

''Don't encourage her,'' he muttered. ''I don't want to go through another day like Monday.''

''What do you mean, another day like Monday?'' He had stopped at the light and she faced him squarely in the darkened interior of the cab. ''You were hardly with her.''

"No, but I had to make that trip from the site to the hospital without knowing how she was doing."

Christine bit her lip, remembering his disheveled appearance when he arrived at the hospital. "They didn't tell you what was the matter?"

"Only that she'd been hurt on the head and taken to the hospital."

The light changed and he edged into the intersection, waiting to make a left turn. The restaurant was on the far side of town, and its parking lot was already full when they pulled in.

Anna raced of ahead of them to the door and Christine took advantage of the opportunity to talk to him without an audience. "Maybe we need to declare a truce," she said quietly.

"A truce? For what?"

He held the door open and she entered the brightly lit room. Voices carried from the dining room into the entryway, and she had to lean toward Jake to hear him.

"For conversation. I mean, we seem to snap at each other every time we talk."

"Doesn't bother me." He gave his name to the hostess, along with a grin that had the young woman smiling back at him before she sashayed toward the dining room.

It wouldn't, Christine thought peevishly as she followed them to their table, listening to him flirt with the hostess. What did it matter if his sister's nurse and babysitter liked him?

She reminded herself she just had to make it through the evening. Once she let him pay for a meal in return for her babysitting, they could go their separate ways. He would feel he had dispatched his obligation and she would have no reason to see him again.

The thought didn't make her feel better. She sat down in a chair on one side of the small table and picked up the large menu, opening it while Anna plopped into the chair on her left and Jake sat down more calmly on her right.

Jake opened his menu. "So, what do we want?"

"I want everything," Anna announced.

He lowered the menu and peered at his sister over the top. "Everything? Even anchovies?"

Anna shook her head. "No."

"Onions?" he asked.

She shook her head again. "No."

"Black olives?"

She chewed on her lower lip. "No."

"Pickles? Bananas? French fries?"

She giggled. "On my pizza? Of course not."

"Mmm." He studied the menu again. "Maybe we should stick with pepperoni."

Anna perched on her knees and studied the menu Christine held. "And salad."

He lowered his menu and grinned at Christine, his eyes twinkling. "Oh, definitely salad. How does that sound to you, Christine?"

Her lips curved upward and she shook her head, closing the menu and laying it at the edge of the table. "Fine." She didn't have a chance against his charm.

The waitress took their order and he leaned back in his chair, resting his arm along the empty chair beside him. "So, how was your day?"

Christine shrugged. "Ordinary. We don't have a lot of action in the hospital, which is fine. A few broken bones from time to time and some stitches. . . ." She smiled at Anna. "The weekends can be busier, and summer brings in the people who have holiday accidents. Other than that, we mainly have people coming in for routine surgeries.''

''Routine surgeries. Isn't that a contradiction in terms?''

''No.'' She sipped at her water and leaned forward, her elbows on the table. ''Gall bladder, tonsils, some appendectomies. A few cases of pneumonia in the winter. Anything more major and we send them to Kansas City. The hospital would like to get another surgeon, but for now, we're lucky with the doctors we have.''

The waitress served their salads. Christine bit back a grin as Anna dove into the fresh vegetables. Her first bite squirted tomato juice on her chin. Jake calmly reached over and wiped it off before unfolding another napkin and draping it on her lap.

''You like what you do?'' he asked, picking up his own fork.

She nodded. ''I always wanted to be a nurse. My favorite Christmas present was a hospital set.''

''Didn't you think about becoming a doctor?''

She was used to the question. ''No. Nursing is just as important, on a different scale. I like being able to give my patients more attention than I could if I were the doctor. Besides, I wanted to stay in Durant and the community can't afford more than a couple of general practitioners and I never wanted to go into surgery.''

When the pizza arrived, he slid a piece onto Anna's plate. She took a bite and spit it out. ''Ouch! It's too hot.''

He rolled the chewed glob into a napkin and tucked it out of sight under the edge of her plate. ''Then blow on it. And don't spit it out again. Do you want Christine to think you have no manners at all?''

''It was too hot,'' she muttered, her head down.

Christine exchanged an amused glance with Jake and

then blew on her own piece of pizza before taking a bite. The cheese seared the inside of her cheek and she bit back an urge to spit it out. She blinked back tears and grabbed her glass, gulping down a big drink.

Jake's expression was mild. His pizza sat on his plate, untouched. He calmly cut off a bite, made a big show of blowing on it, and stuck it in his mouth. "Hmm," he mumbled over the bite.

Christine deliberately turned away from him. After a few moments, she cut off a bite of pizza and slowly put it in her mouth. This time, she had the satisfaction of tasting the spicy flavors without the pain.

He kept them entertained with stories about his building crew, Anna chiming in with details that let Christine know she was often on the building sites. The pizza disappeared while she listened. When the last bite had been swallowed, Anna jumped to her feet and raced to Jake's side, her hand out.

He dug in his pocket and extracted two bills. "This is all you get," he warned her.

She nodded and, clutching the money in her hand, headed for the game room. "She'll either come right back with a forlorn look on her face, or we'll be here all night," he told Christine. "The first time we came, she used her money in about five minutes. I had told her that was it, but I don't think she believed me. When she saw she couldn't get more from whining, she started to cry. We just walked out. The next time, she took forever to spend her tokens."

"You don't have any kids of your own hidden away, do you?" Christine asked. She leaned back in her chair while the waitress cleared the table.

"Not that I know of." He hooked his arm over the back

of the empty chair, his legs stretched out next to Christine's. "Why?"

"You're pretty good at this parenting business."

"Really? I thought you were ready to turn me in."

She gave an exasperated sigh. "You know what, Jake, I made an error in judgment. You could be a neater housekeeper, but Anna looks like she's doing fine."

She came tearing back to the table just then, her hair flying behind her. A slightly older boy was right behind her. "You owe me a quarter!" he shouted.

Anna ducked behind Christine, her face crushed against Christine's shoulder. Christine instinctively reached behind and pressed her hand over Anna's head. "What's the matter?"

"She hit my arm while I was playing Battlestar. My rocket exploded and I lost my turn." The boy advanced on Anna, thunder in his eyes.

Jake stopped him with a firm hand. "Anna, look at me."

Anna peeped out from her safety spot. "Did you bump him?"

"It was an accident," she said.

Jake's eyes narrowed. "I wanted to play," she said after a moment.

"Give me the tokens you have left."

"No." She pressed against Christine's side again.

"Anna." Christine shifted in her chair until she was facing the little girl. "Give your brother your tokens."

"No." She kept her head turned away from them.

Christine was aware of the curious glances of the other diners, many of them familiar faces. She gave an inward groan. She wouldn't have to tell her mother about her dinner with Jake. The neighbors would do it for her.

"Anna, that's one," Jake said quietly.

Christine felt the quiver and then Anna slipped her hand into her pocket. Three slim golden coins stamped with the restaurant's name clanked into Jake's hand.

He handed them to the boy. "Sorry. Maybe you can save the galaxy this time."

The boy stared at the tokens and then lifted his head. "I only lost one quarter."

"You might as well use them all," Jake said, standing up. "We're going home."

Anna didn't say a word as they walked back to the car. When Jake walked around the truck, she kept her hands firmly tucked in her lap, her chin pressed against her chest.

"Well, that was a perfect ending," he said when he climbed in.

"I'm sorry, Jake." Her voice was pitiful. Christine barely resisted the urge to wrap her arm around the stubborn shoulders.

"You should be telling the boy. You ruined his game, not mine."

A sniffle drifted from under the curtain of dark hair. "I didn't mean to."

"Anna." He pulled into the traffic.

"Well, he was taking too long. I put my token on the machine but he kept taking one out of his pocket and putting it in the slot."

Jake shifted and glanced at her. "He did?"

Anna nodded her head. "He didn't have another token on the machine when I put mine there. But he put three more in."

Jake lifted one hand from the steering wheel and rubbed his chin. "Well, bumping his arm wasn't right, but he wasn't playing fair either." He reached over and chucked

Anna under the chin. "You've had enough punishment for tonight. Okay?"

She nodded, her lips curving upward in a faint smile. Jake ran his finger over her cheek and then moved his hand back to the steering wheel.

Something lurched in the pit of Christine's stomach. His gentle gesture with his sister, his sense of fair play, all added to an attractive picture that she didn't want to carry around. It was easier when they were sparring with each other. This soft side of Jake bothered her and made her think about things she didn't want to consider.

He pulled into her driveway and she jumped out before he could come around and open her door. He quirked one eyebrow when he met her at the front of the truck. "I was going to open your door," he said.

"That's okay," she said breezily. "It's not like this was a date or anything."

"No." He fell into step with her and walked her to the front door.

She turned toward him, her hand already rummaging in her purse for her key. The outside light she had left on bathed them in a pale yellow circle. A breeze whipped her hair around her cheeks, a cool reminder of autumn's arrival. "Thanks for dinner. I guess we're even now."

He jammed his hands into the back pockets of his jeans. "Yeah, I guess we are." He didn't move, even when she opened the door.

She paused, one hand on the knob. Behind her, she could hear Rocky's whimpering. "Well, good night."

"Good night."

For a moment, she thought he was going to kiss her. She leaned toward him a fraction, her lips aching for the touch of his, and then he stepped off the narrow porch and onto the flagstone. "I'll see you around."

She stepped into the house and shut the door, leaning against its sturdy frame. Her heart pounded under her sweater and she pressed a fisted hand to her chest. It continued its quick thud as the truck roared to life and then disappeared down the street.

"I'll see you around." Not a single promise in the casual words.

With a mental kick for herself, she hung her jacket in the closet and went into the kitchen to feed Rocky. At least she knew where she stood with the puppy.

Chapter Four

She was filling in again for Emily two days later when she heard a familiar voice. "Hi, Miss Hunter, I'm back."

Christine leaned over the counter and smiled at Anna. Her bangs were still shaggy, but they had grown enough to cover the stitches. "Hi. Are you here to take out the stitches or get new ones?"

Anna giggled. "Take out the old ones."

Christine glanced around, but she didn't see Jake. An older woman Christine vaguely recognized stood behind Anna, one hand lightly resting on the little shoulder. "I'm Rita Anderson," she said. "Mr. Reynolds had to go out of town so he asked me to bring his sister in today. He gave me his insurance card and a note with his signature."

Work again, Christine thought, clicking a button on her computer. "That's fine."

A few minutes later, Christine walked into the emergency room area with Anna and their neighbor. From Anna's chatter, she discovered that the woman watched

44

Anna whenever Jake thought he'd be home later than the required closing time of the after-school program.

"Your brother coaches the track team, right?" Rita asked as Christine helped Anna onto the examining table.

"My brother Luke does."

"My grandson runs on the team. He thinks the world of your brother."

That would explain the feeling of familiarity. She attended most of the local track meets to support her brother and the team. "Luke does a good job."

Christine gently probed the area around the stitches, satisfied the wound was healing nicely. "Looks good. You shouldn't have much of a scar. It will practically disappear."

"No scar?"

Christine grinned at the disappointment in Anna's voice. "Oh, but it won't disappear before Halloween," she informed her.

"Really?"

Her smile broadened at the bright look on Anna's face. "Really."

Lifting the loose bangs, she snipped the neat stitches and gently tugged them out. "All done." She helped Anna back to the floor and brushed her tousled bangs into place.

The sides of Anna's hair weren't as jagged as the fringe over her eyebrows, but they were definitely in need of a trim. Glancing at the clock, Christine made an impulsive decision. "Would you like to get a haircut? One that doesn't involve school scissors?"

"Oh, yeah!" Anna frowned. "But Jake said he wouldn't be home until bedtime."

"We don't need to wait for Jake." Christine smiled at

Mrs. Anderson. "I get off in an hour. I could pick her up, take her to the beauty shop, and then stay with her until Jake gets home."

"Well . . ." Mrs. Anderson hesitated, her face clearly showing her uncertainty.

A pang flitted through Christine. Jake hadn't mentioned her to his regular sitter. *Not that he needed to,* she reminded herself. *I was just a quick-fix situation.*

"It's okay," Anna piped up. "Christine watched me the day I got stitches. Jake gave her a key to the house and everything."

"Oh?" Mrs. Anderson was looking at Christine with curiosity now.

Christine flushed under the intent gaze. "I left the key at his house that night."

"I have one," Mrs. Anderson said, accepting Christine's offer. "I'll give it to you when you pick up Anna. I'm the house on the north side of theirs."

"I'll see you after I get off work then."

After they left, Christine went back to the nurse's station in the center of the emergency room. With the hospital short-handed, she had been helping on the other floors when her regular hours permitted. No paperwork marred the neat desk top. She drummed her fingers on the smooth finishing, wondering when the listlessness had invaded. She loved nursing and had meant every word she had told Jake the other day about her career decision. But she was finding it harder to be completely satisfied with her life at the end of each day.

She started to head home after her shift and decided to stop by Mrs. Anderson's house first. Anna could play with Rocky in the backyard while she changed clothes and looked through her mail. As soon as she opened the door,

Anna raced into the house and kept up the same pace as she ran into the fenced yard after Rocky.

Her regular hairdresser had an opening in thirty minutes and said she would be delighted to repair Anna's foray into hair design. Christine pulled on a pair of jeans and a blue top embroidered with bright butterflies, listening to Rocky's excited yipping and Anna's giggles. She smiled. It was hard to stay down when the leaves were changing colors, a little girl was chasing a puppy in the backyard, and butterflies were flitting over her shoulders.

She stood in the back door and watched Rocky jump at Anna's legs, his already big paws scraping down her shins. Anna spun away from him, a stick held high above her head. "Come on, Rocky!" she urged the dog. "Fetch!"

She tossed the stick toward the corner of the yard and clapped her hands together when Rocky snatched it between his teeth and brought it back to her. They engaged in a friendly game of tug-of-war until Anna succeeded in prying it away from him.

They tossed it several more times before Christine made her presence known. "We need to go," she called to Anna. "Liz is going to squeeze you in between a perm and a highlight."

"Okay." Anna twirled around as she ran toward the back door, leaping and hopping over the excited puppy.

Rocky whimpered when Christine secured him behind the gate. Anna bent over and petted his head. "I'll come back and play, boy," she assured him.

She dropped into the front seat of Christine's car. "I wish we had a dog."

"They take a lot of work." Christine turned the key and drove toward the main part of town.

"That's what Jake always says. He says a dog wouldn't

get any attention because we're hardly home. But you work all day and you have a dog.''

Christine nodded. ''True, but I don't work every day.''

''Jake doesn't have to.'' Anna scrunched down in her seat, her chin on her chest. ''Sometimes I think he'd rather build a house than be with me.''

Christine could hear the pain in her little voice. She didn't know Jake's true feelings, but she didn't like the lost sound echoing in her car. ''Anna, your brother cares about you very much. And I thought you liked going to the sites with him.''

''I do. But he only lets me go on the weekends. I have to stay with Mrs. Anderson or at the after-school program on the other days.''

They arrived at the beauty salon and Christine waited while Anna unbuckled her seat belt. ''I had to do the same thing with my dad,'' said Christine. ''He worked at the fire station and I never got to go down there during a school day.''

''Your dad works at the fire station?''

Christine held the door open. The odors of hair color, perms, and potpourri spilled into the fresh air. The clatter of scissors and curling irons vied with the chatter from the customers and stylists. ''Not anymore. He retired a year ago.''

''Oh.'' Anna's shoulders drooped as she crossed the patterned carpet. ''I thought maybe he could show me around the fire station. The kids in my class went last year in first grade, but I didn't live here then.''

Christine bent down until her lips were only inches away from Anna's ears. ''I bet Dad could still arrange a personal tour,'' she whispered.

Anna straightened so quickly, Christine had to jump back

to miss having her head cracked. "Really? Cool. Wait 'til the kids hear about this."

"Just don't tell them until I work it out."

Following Anna toward the reception desk, she wondered what she was doing. Her initial interest in the little girl was quickly turning into something more. She hated seeing those narrow shoulders droop. If she wasn't careful, she would find every free moment tied up with a seven-year-old.

And what would be wrong with that? she asked herself as she picked up a magazine and settled into a cushioned chair in the waiting area. Liz had agreed that a blunt shoulder cut with a fringe of bangs would be just right for Anna's hair and face shape. Anna had hopped onto the box Liz had placed on the chair and was chatting away as if she had known Liz for decades instead of just minutes.

Are you doing it for Anna or because of her brother? That little girl has had enough trouble in her young life without getting new friends because of her fascinating brother.

Christine stared unseeingly at the magazine open on her lap. She had never spent so much time analyzing her decisions. From the day she had received her first medical kit, she had been set on a career as a nurse, picking her high school courses with that goal in sight, never wavering until she had her nursing degree in hand. Not once had she considered practicing anywhere besides Durant, seeing her return to the community as a thank you for its support during her growing-up years.

Maybe that's the problem, she thought now. *After Mandy went away for a few years, she knew this was where she wanted to be. Even Jake took a while before he settled here. Maybe I need to see more of the world.*

She didn't have time for any more thinking. "Look, Christine, look!"

Anna's voice bounced off the ceiling and walls of the small building. Christine folded her magazine and made her way through the chairs until she stood next to Anna.

"Wow!" Christine smiled at Liz's reflection in the mirror. "You're great."

"Thanks." Liz fluffed the softened ends of Anna's bangs and gave the shortened ends over her right shoulder another quick twist with the curling iron. "She has lovely hair."

Anna twisted her head back and forth, watching the ends drop back into place. "I can't even mess it up."

Christine and Liz both laughed. "I bet you will," Liz said, untying the cape from around Anna's neck and brushing loose hairs onto the floor. "But just wash it, brush it, and you're ready to go. You don't have to curl it unless you want to."

Anna hopped down from the chair. "Now I don't have to use all those barrettes and things Jake always wants to buy me."

"Probably a good thing," Christine said, remembering their exchange in the emergency room.

They stopped at the grocery store on the way home, picking up ingredients for a casserole and salad. Anna chatted with the produce manager, carefully studying the fruits as he named them. He picked up a slender green fruit, slicing off a piece and showing her the star shape of the citrus fruit.

"Can we buy one?" Anna asked after she tasted it.

Christine nodded and dropped one in the basket. "But if we don't get home soon, you'll be eating supper at bedtime."

Anna perched on a high stool in the small kitchen and

helped Christine add the vegetables together, sharing high-lights of her school day as she popped pea pods open. Once the casserole was in the oven, she ran outside with Rocky, throwing sticks until it was too dark to see. The oven timer dinged as she came into the house. She hurried over to the stove, standing on tiptoe as Christine took the hot dish out of the oven.

"It smells good."

Christine carefully lowered the steaming pan onto a hot pad on the counter. "It looks good, too."

Juices bubbled on the top and the leftover mashed potatoes she had used for frosting were lightly browned. She opened the cupboard and took down two plates, handing them to Anna just as the doorbell rang.

"I'll get it!" Anna sang out, racing toward the living room before Christine could move.

She placed the plates on the table and followed at a slower pace. Her brothers were notorious for showing up at dinnertime, and she expected to see one of them standing on the front porch.

She didn't expect to see Jake, a thunderous look on his face. "Finally!" he snapped.

"We just heard the doorbell," she said, puzzled by his animosity. Anna held the doorknob with both hands, her brows drawn together.

"I've been looking all over for you," he told Anna.

"Didn't Mrs. Anderson tell you she was with me?" Christine asked.

"She's not home." He strode into the room, his arms crossed over his chest. "I thought maybe she had taken Anna to our house, but the house is dark. So I checked the pizza place. No luck. They weren't at the burger joint either. I decided that since she had her stitches out today, maybe you would have an idea where she was. I should have known I'd find her here.''

"Now wait a minute . . ." Christine paused, aware that Anna was watching the interchange with wide, curious eyes.

She took a deep breath. "Have you eaten?"

"What?"

"Have you eaten?" she repeated slowly.

"No. I hurried back to town so I could see Anna."

So he hadn't deserted her completely. Christine turned toward the kitchen. "Anna and I just finished cooking a casserole. You're welcome to join us."

She didn't wait to see if he would accept the invitation, but she could hear his footsteps behind her as she entered the kitchen. She took down another plate, added glasses to her collection, and carried the dishes to the table set in the small bay window that overlooked the side yard. Working quickly, she added the other dishes and then carried the casserole to the center of the table.

Anna brought out the salad they had put together. She carefully layered pieces of star fruit around the perimeter of the bowl. She sat down in the chair closest to Rocky's corner of the kitchen. "You can't feed him table scraps," Christine said.

"I won't," Anna promised. "I just like looking at him."

Christine grinned and poured cold water into the glasses. "Lemon?" she asked, holding a slice over each glass.

"Cool!" Anna knelt on her chair and squeezed lemon juice into her water. "This is just like a restaurant."

"Not quite," Christine said, pleased by the compliment. Her home economics teacher had always stressed that the presentation was as important as the menu and didn't require a lot of extra effort.

"I'll pass on the lemon." Jake sat down opposite his sister and drained his glass of water with one gulp. Christine refilled it without a word.

While they ate, Anna told Jake about their shopping expedition and how they had prepared the dinner. Christine ate silently, waiting for him to comment on his sister's new hairdo. When they had finished the main course and a dessert of ice cream and cookies, Anna asked to be excused. "Can I take Rocky outside? I won't run around."

Christine started to answer and then looked at Jake. "Do you mind?"

"No." He turned to Anna. "But we can't stay long. I want to be at the job site as soon as the sun comes up tomorrow."

"Okay." Anna freed Rocky from his pen and the door slammed shut behind them.

"I'm sorry about the mix-up," Christine said, carrying dishes to the sink.

"I didn't mean to snap at you." Jake handed her the dessert dishes. "That was very good, by the way. No matter what Anna says, that beats restaurant food all to pieces."

Warmth crept up Christine's neck at the compliment. The simplicity impressed her more than flowery words would have done. "Thank you. Anna helped."

He grinned. "I know. I bet I could figure out exactly which peas she added."

Christine chuckled. "She does go into detail, doesn't she?"

They finished the dishes in a companionable silence, Jake wiping down the table while she added dishwasher soap to the machine. She kept the door ajar, planning to run it when she was alone.

Jake sat down at the table and she took the chair across

from him. "Thanks for watching her," he said. "I didn't expect you to do it."

"I don't mind." She folded her hands on top of the table. "Actually, it was my idea. How did you like her new haircut?"

He frowned. "Her new haircut? I didn't notice."

Christine gave an exasperated sigh. "How could you not notice? It's at least three inches shorter and her bangs are even."

He lifted his hands toward her, palms up. "Sorry. Now, if she had new siding or her shutters had been painted. . . ."

"You're impossible, Jake. No wonder my mom would get so frustrated with my brothers."

"Hey! Don't lump all us men together."

"Why not? You have this darling little girl and you don't even realize it."

He leaned forward, his elbows on the table and his chin propped on his hands. "Are you saying she should be wearing frilly dresses and playing with dolls again?"

"No, I'm not!" She put her elbows on the table and laced her fingers together before resting her chin on them, meeting his gaze easily. "But you could tell she wanted you to notice her hair and you didn't say a thing."

"Why didn't you give me a hint?"

"Why should I do all your work for you?"

He leaned back in his chair. "Hey, I didn't ask you to butt in."

"Somebody had to. I never saw anybody so excited by a trip to the grocery store. She wanted to know what everything was."

"So I don't take her shopping!" He ran his hand through his hair. "You know, we were doing pretty well before you came along."

"Right. She was cutting her own hair with a pair of school scissors. The kitchen floor looked like the bottom of a pigpen and the only edible food came out of a box." She nodded, crossing her arms over her chest. "You were doing great."

He surprised her by laughing. "That was good."

"What?"

"You never gave an inch. I bet you could go on all night."

She smiled. "My brothers are physically stronger, so I had to develop another talent. I don't think they ever got the last word after I turned eight."

"They have my sympathy." He extended a hand. "Could we start over, please?"

Her anatomy instructor had taught her the bones of the hand, the ligaments that held the bones together, the various muscles. She had watched surgeons with long, delicate hands carefully work on a body, and she had cleaned scrapes and cuts on big hands and little hands. But no hand had affected her the way Jake's did.

Calluses brushed against the sensitive skin of her palm. His hand was warm and when she wrapped her fingers around it, she could feel the wiry hairs that grew on the back. His thumb gently caressed the tender skin between her finger and thumb. She shivered slightly before carefully pulling her hand out of his grasp.

"I—it's getting late," she managed. "I am working tomorrow."

He shoved his chair back from the table and stood up. "I promised Anna I'd take her to the site in the morning," he said gruffly.

He paused at the edge of the table. Time stopped for a moment as she looked into his eyes. She tipped her head and watched as he slowly lowered his head. She waited, her gaze following his mouth as it descended to hers.

His lips were warm and dry. The kiss only lasted a few seconds, a short, sweet whisper that sent currents of longing through her.

"Good night," he murmured against her lips, his breath mingling with hers. "And thank you again."

Her eyes opened slowly as he shifted away from her. Her bones had melted and she knew that she would stumble if she stood up. As if through a foggy window, she watched him open the back door and call Anna inside. He scooped up the puppy as he ran past and deposited him behind the gate before shutting the door.

"Tell Christine thank you," he instructed Anna.

She raced to Christine's side. "Thank you." She wrapped her arms around her neck. Christine was grateful to find she had regained enough energy to return the hug.

A sloppy kiss landed in the vicinity of her cheek. "See you later, alligator," Anna sang as she ran toward the front door.

Jake chuckled and shook his head. "If my crew had half her energy, the house would be done."

He bent down and gave her a swift kiss, standing up before she could react. "I'll call you later." His long stride ate up the distance between the table and the arch. "Anna, wait for me."

Bemused, she listened to the front door close and his truck start up. When the last rev of the motor disappeared into the distance, she stood up and walked over to the counter, pushing the dishwasher door closed before patting Rocky good night. "I'm not sure I can sleep," she told the drowsy puppy. "But I sure hope I dream."

Chapter Five

Christine dropped the box she was carrying in the only open space on the living room floor. "Here you go, Rebecca." She slowly turned around the small room, its normally neat area covered with stacks of boxes. "What do you need these for anyway?"

The older woman knelt in front of a box and carefully pried it open. "My women's group is having a rummage sale next week to raise money for Thanksgiving baskets. I thought I'd go through the attic and see what I could give away." She tugged open a box and pulled out a thick sweater crocheted with butterflies. "I can't believe how much I've collected over the years."

"This is pretty." Christine smoothed her hand over the sweater Rebecca was holding. "I like butterflies."

"Do you? Here." Rebecca draped the sweater over Christine's arm. "For helping."

Christine lifted her hands, backing away from the sweater. "I wasn't hinting, Rebecca. Besides, I'd be happy to buy it at the sale." She nudged a heavy box with the

57

toe of her shoe. "You know, Dr. Sanders wouldn't be happy to know you were planning to carry this down yourself."

Rebecca studied a colorful painting from several angles and then dropped it back into its box. "I was fine. Why Mandy had to drag you out of bed and over here . . ."

"She didn't drag me out of bed and you know it." Christine perched on the armrest of the couch, a grin on her face. "She was going to come herself, but she already promised Jessie they would go shopping."

"Isn't she the sweetest thing? I think Mandy married Greg as much to be that little girl's mother as for him."

Christine turned an interested eye on her older friend. "Really?"

"Well," Rebecca opened another box and sifted through its contents, adding two tea towels and a set of mugs with floral designs to the small pile on her left. "I wouldn't say it to Mandy, but I think knowing Jessie came with the package helped."

"Hmmm." Christine slid onto a cushion, her elbow on her knee and her chin resting on her fisted hand. "You don't think Mandy would have married Greg otherwise?"

"Oh, no, I didn't mean that at all." Rebecca shook her head at Christine. "Greg and Mandy love each other very much. It just helps that Mandy and Jessie get along so well. And she is a darling girl. Who wouldn't want to be her mother? But a child needs two parents who love each other just as much as they love the child. Jessie has that now, at least with her father. I don't know about her mother."

"But you said—"

"I know what I said," Rebecca interrupted, joining Christine on the couch. She draped the butterfly sweater over Christine's lap. "What I meant is that seeing Greg with Jessie helped Mandy know what he would be like with their own children.''

Like Jake and Anna, Christine thought as she drove back to town. *He's firm but calm.* That side of him was very appealing. She wondered if that was how Mandy had felt when she was first around Greg and his daughter.

A light breeze from the open car window tossed her hair around her face. The day was balmy, a pleasant reprieve before the winter came in. She veered toward Mandy's house and slowed down as she approached the comfortable ranch home that Greg had bought shortly after his move to Durant. The house was pleasantly situated on a quiet street not far from the hospital. Christine could see the changes Mandy had initiated since her spring wedding, but she understood her friend's desire to have a place that would be their own. And with the new baby on the way, and probably one or two more after that, the house would become rather tight.

The car her friend typically used was in the driveway and she pulled in behind it. Voices sounded from the backyard. She made her way around the side yard, pausing at the chain-link fence that delineated their property.

Leaves dotted the grass and, while she stood there, several more floated down from the neighbor's oak tree. A cardinal flew past her head into the branches of a tree at the back of the yard, its red feathers brilliant against the still green grass. Mandy and her new daughter were pulling weeds from the flowerbed next to the back door. Jessie's head bobbed up and down as she talked, her little face animated.

''Hi.'' Christine reached over and pulled the latch on the gate, letting herself in.

Mandy sat back on her heels. "Hi. Did you get Granny squared away?"

Christine nodded, advancing toward them. "How long has it been since she cleaned that attic? I thought we'd get lost in there."

"I don't know." Mandy grinned. "Did you make a dent?"

"Hardly. The boxes multiplied while we were carrying them downstairs. Her living room floor is packed, but you can barely see a difference in the attic."

"Wait until you see how little she gives away." Mandy shook her head, a tolerant grin on her face. "She'll remember a story or an incident and end up packing the boxes up again and carrying them back upstairs."

Christine chuckled. "Her pile wasn't much bigger than your weed pile."

"Hey!" Mandy dropped another green stalk on the small pile between them. "I'll have you know, we're about worn out from weeding, aren't we, Jessie?"

The little girl nodded, her ponytail flopping against her shoulders. "I think I have a blister." She held her gloved hand toward Christine.

"Should we go to the emergency room?" Christine asked "Or maybe the thumb store?"

Jessie giggled. "There isn't a thumb store!"

Christine leaned back, her eyes and mouth wide. "There isn't?"

Mandy tugged at Jessie's ponytail, her expression softening. "Why don't you give your gloves to Christine and go see if Megan can play? You've done a lot today."

"Gee, thanks, Mom!" Jessie stripped off her gloves and dropped them at Christine's feet. "Bye!"

Mandy's glow didn't diminish as she watched the little

girl run off. Christine wondered how long it had taken for Mandy to become close to Jessie. Her own feelings toward Anna grew every time she was with her and she knew if they ever found themselves separated for a long period of time, she would miss her.

The gate clattered shut. "She's so cheerful all the time," Christine said.

"Most of the time," Mandy corrected. "Bedtime can be tricky."

Christine knelt down and tugged a weed away from a geranium. The flower's bright color echoed that of the cardinal that had flashed by. "Does it ever bother you that you're not really her mother?"

Mandy glanced over her shoulder at Christine, her eyes narrowed. "No. She's part of my family now. I didn't ask her to call me Mom, she just started it herself. She doesn't see Susan that often so I don't feel like I'm hurting anyone."

"You're probably helping her," Christine murmured. "Filling a void she has."

"I guess so. I'd rather think I'm creating a place of my own within her heart." Mandy rocked back on her heels, her hands crossed over her knees. "What's this all about, Christine? Are you . . ." She broke off, her eyes widening. "Jake!"

Christine could feel her cheeks go warm. "What do you mean?"

"You're wondering what it's like to fall for a guy who has a child already."

"I'm not falling for him, Mandy. You make me sound like a teenager."

Mandy grinned. "Do you feel like one?"

Christine shook her head and then remembered the sleepless nights, the tingling she had felt in her stomach just before he kissed her, the number of times she had traced her finger over her lips. "Maybe. But I don't even know if we're going anywhere. I mean, he took me out once, with his sister," she added quickly when she saw the interested look in Mandy's face—"and he's been to the house for dinner. Again, with his sister."

"That's good, though. He doesn't mind you being around his sister." Mandy tossed a weed onto the pile that had rapidly been growing while they talked and worked. "Now if he kisses you. . . ."

She lifted her head and grinned. "He's kissed you, hasn't he?"

Christine hesitated, wondering if her friend could really tell, and then nodded. She wanted to talk about him, to find out what she was feeling, to see if she was being crazy or if she should just slow down. "After dinner last week. Just once, but . . ."

"But you had trouble sleeping," Mandy supplied.

"I kept thinking I would go to sleep and dream about it but every time I closed my eyes, I could feel his lips touching mine." She closed her eyes and sighed before opening them again. "I've got it bad, don't I?"

"He's a nice guy, Christine. And even though Anna has been in some trouble at school, I think she's a sweetheart."

"Anna is in trouble at school?" Christine paused, her hands on the dirt in front of her. "What kind of trouble?"

Mandy shrugged. "She's not in my class so I don't know all the details, but she's been to the office a few times."

"Are you sure it's Anna?"

"Yeah. I had to go to the work room the other day to make some copies, and she was sitting in a chair by the principal's office, kicking her feet back and forth. She had this big scowl on her face.''

''I can't believe this.'' Christine pushed herself to her feet and paced up and down the small sidewalk. ''When she's at my house, she's so sweet. She talks a lot, but she always follows directions. And Rocky loves her.''

Mandy dusted off her hands and sat back on her heels. ''Some of her trouble may be related to adjusting to a new school. It can't be easy for her, losing her mom and her dad like she did. She's been through a lot in the last few months.''

''True.'' Christine leaned against the side of the porch railing and toyed with a loose string on her right glove. She tugged it free and wrapped it around her index fingers, twisting it back and forth. ''So, what can I do?''

''Sounds like you're already doing what you can. She needs a friend, Christine, somebody who cares about her.''

''I can do that.''

Mandy scooped the weeds into her arms and stood up. ''Now about her brother,'' she said, striding toward the back corner of the yard. ''We need to get the two of you together without Anna around. I'd be happy to have her come over here, if that would help.''

''What?''

''You need some time alone with Jake, to see if you really do have any chemistry. You could ask him out.''

''Mandy!'' She lifted her hands and yelped when the string tightened around her fingers. Mandy was sitting on the porch by the time she untangled herself.

''I can't ask Jake out.''

''Why not?'' Mandy perched on the porch railing, one foot swinging back and forth. ''A woman can ask a man out, you know.''

"I know, but what would we do?"

"What does he like to do?"

Christine shook her head. "I don't know. We've usually talked about Anna or our work." *Or argued about how he cares for Anna*, she thought. But Mandy didn't need to know that. She'd probably read something into that conversation, too. "I don't know what kind of movies he likes or if he even likes movies. All I really know is that he played football."

"Then ask him to a football game."

Christine imagined all the people that would be sitting in the stands, their attention torn between the action on the field and the couple sitting in the middle of them. She wasn't ready for that kind of scrutiny. "I don't think a football game would work."

Mandy was silent, her lips pressed together before she nodded in agreement. "You're probably right. He'd be more interested in watching the game than talking to you. And movies wouldn't give you much time to talk either."

She chewed on her lower lip. "You need someplace where you can talk without being in the middle of a crowd."

Christine waited, recognizing the intent look on her friend's face. She could almost see the wheels turning before Mandy's face lit up. "I know. Ask him to a track meet."

Christine considered the suggestion for a moment before giving a slight shrug. "I could do that."

"Really?" Her foot slowed and Mandy tipped her head, a suspicious look on her face. "Wait a minute, why the sudden agreement?"

Christine bit back a grin. She and Mandy had been friends too long. They could read each other's expressions and faces better than anyone. "I was just thinking that in six or seven months, I could probably get up the courage to ask him out."

"Six or seven months! That'll be spring."

"I know." Christine linked her hands together over one knee and leaned back on the step. Her lips curved upward as she smiled at Mandy. "That is the season for track."

Mandy stared at her for a moment and then laughed. "Okay, not track. What is it Luke is coaching right now?"

"Now?" Christine glanced at the sky, scratching her head as if she couldn't remember.

"Yes, now." Mandy gave her a light punch. "Don't they have some kind of running events going on right now?"

"Some kind of running events?" Christine echoed. "Do you know what Luke would say if he heard you?"

"I don't care." Mandy leaned forward, her face only inches away from Christine. "You're being deliberately stubborn. If I didn't know better, I'd say you were scared of being alone with Jake."

Mandy was absolutely right. Just standing in the doorway with him had sent her heart shooting right down to her feet and then rocketing back up again. She couldn't imagine what would happen if she spent any length of time alone with him.

"It's not so much scared—" she began.

"Scared," Mandy interrupted. She rested her hand on Christine's arm. "It's okay, I've been there. You're afraid your whole life will be turned upside down. But trust me, it's worth it."

"But how do I know Jake is even interested in me?"

"Ask him out."

Christine shook her head at her friend's persistence. "I am not going to ask him out. I've never asked a guy out."

"Really? No wonder you stay home so many nights."

Christine stared at her. Mandy's lips curved upward in a broad grin. "Thank you very much, *friend*," she said, with heavy emphasis on the last word.

"Come on, Christine, why not? You like him, don't you? And he doesn't have a serious girlfriend right now."

The picture of Marilyn at the restaurant came to mind, but she remembered that the other woman had been the one to state that she liked mixing business with pleasure. Jake hadn't said anything, and he hadn't seemed interested in Marilyn in a more personal way. Or was that just wishful thinking?

She sighed. "I don't know, Mandy, it just seems so—pushy."

"Christine, you, pushy?" Mandy's bark of laughter frightened a squirrel that was foraging in a bush next to the house. It scurried over the fence into the neighbor's yard. "Honey, you would never be considered pushy."

"Thank you, I think." She rubbed her clasped hands over her chin. "So, you think I should ask him out."

"What do you have to lose?" Mandy said.

Only my self-esteem, Christine thought several hours later, sitting alone at home. She stared at the telephone receiver and dropped it back into the cradle. She couldn't call him up. As long as she didn't make the call, she wouldn't be rejected.

He could accept, she reminded herself, picking up the phone again. *But if you don't call, you'll never know.*

The phone rang fifteen times before she hung up. "I thought he'd have an answering machine," she told Rocky. "Of course, I wouldn't know what to say to one." The puppy lifted his head and watched her for a moment before returning his attention to a rawhide bone. His teeth scraped against the stiff material.

The shrill bell of the phone jangled and she jumped, pressing her hand against her heart. She waited for her pulse to slow down before picking it up. "So, what happened?" Mandy asked from the other end.

"I haven't asked him yet."

"Christine, come on. Do you want your life just to pass you by?"

She propped her stockinged feet on the coffee table. "I tried, Mandy, but he wasn't home."

"Oh."

Rocky padded over and rested his head on her elevated legs. She scratched behind his ears and grinned as he thumped the floor with one foot. "Did you ever ask Greg out?"

"No. But that's just because we ended up together on our own without any help from me."

"Well, maybe we will, too. We just met, you know."

A sigh sounded from the other end of the phone. "Christine, you and Jake have been in this town for years. At this rate, Anna will have children of her own before you two get together. If you ever do."

"If it's supposed to happen, it will," Christine said stubbornly.

"Ask him out," Mandy warned, "or I'll get you together on my own."

Muttering curses against meddling best friends, Christine hung up the phone. She didn't doubt Mandy would do something. She seldom missed a chance to help her friends. Christine knew that if Mandy hadn't pushed her to talk to the boy who sat in front of her in calculus, she would never have gone to the prom with him. After studying together for a month, he had casually mentioned the prom and before she went home that night, she had eagerly agreed to go as his date and had even experienced her first kiss.

She traced a finger over her lips, comparing that kiss with the one Jake had given her. Her first kiss had been intense, a crushing of lips just before he ran out the door. His goodnight kiss the night of the prom had been even more desperate, the force practically impaling her teeth against her lips.

But Jake's kiss. . . . She sighed and leaned back in her chair, reliving again the way he had gently touched her mouth with his and then built up the intensity degree by degree, taking her with him each pulse-pounding step. The man knew how to kiss. The kiss had only lasted a few seconds, but she had felt it to the tips of her toes and still, days later, she could feel the imprint against her lips.

She sat up and straightened her shoulders, reaching for the phone. She wasn't a teenager anymore, willing to moon over a boy from a distance. If Jake was interested, he would accept her date. If not, she would at least know where she stood and she could go on from there.

The phone rang four times before it was answered. "Hello, Reynolds residence. Anna speaking."

Anna. For a moment, Christine faltered. What would happen to her relationship with Anna if Jake didn't go out with her? Would he refuse to let them be together? Mandy had said the little girl needed a friend. Would she feel betrayed if Christine quit seeing her? And how would she feel?

"Hello?" Anna said again. "Who's calling, please?"

Christine swallowed. "Hi, Anna, it's Christine."

"Hi, Christine. We just got back from the job site. You

should see how dirty I am.'' A giggle traveled over the line.

''Are you going to take a bath?''

''Nope.'' Another giggle. ''I'm going to take a shower!''

Whoops sounded from Anna's end of the line and Christine could almost see her holding her middle and laughing. This was the same little girl who was getting in trouble at school? Surely Mandy was mistaken.

Christine grinned. ''Have fun. Could I talk to Jake while you're showering?''

''Sure.''

She cleared her throat while she waited for Jake to come on the line. Her hands felt clammy. She wiped them, one at a time, on her jeans. She was taking a deep breath when she heard his hello.

''Hi.'' Her voice came out in a rush and she swallowed, trying again. ''How are you, Jake?''

''Fine. Anna said you wanted to talk to me.''

''Yes.'' Now that he was on the line, she didn't know how to start. ''She said she got dirty at the site.''

''Yeah. A couple kids from her class live nearby and the three of them discovered the huge pile of dirt that came from the foundation hole. I hope their parents are understanding.''

''Kids come in wash and wear, don't they?''

He laughed, the deep sound sliding down her spine. ''I think so.'' A pause and then, ''So, did you call for any special reason?''

Her courage trickled back in. ''I was wondering, that is, my brother Luke coaches the cross-country team and I thought, maybe, if you weren't busy next Saturday . . .''

''We could watch the meet?'' he finished for her when she paused.

"Yes."

"I'll have to check my calendar but I suppose I could take off a few hours. I'm not sure Anna would want to stand around that long, though."

Christine breathed a tiny sigh of relief for Mandy's foresight. "She probably would get bored," she said carefully. "I'm sure my friend Mandy Sanders wouldn't mind watching her. She has a stepdaughter about a year younger than Anna."

"That sounds great."

She gave him directions to Mandy's house, and then they made arrangements to meet at the high school parking lot and ride together to the golf course where the meets were held. She hung up the phone and twirled around the room several times before dropping to the floor in front of a curious Rocky.

She cupped her hands around the puppy's face. "It may not be the most exciting date, Rocky, but I made it myself. Who knows what can happen now?"

Chapter Six

"I can't believe I'm doing this," she muttered to Rocky, tossing a sweater onto the rapidly growing pile on her bed. "You'd think I'd never gone out before. How much more of a cliché can I be, searching for the perfect outfit?"

Rocky cocked his head, his dark eyes glittering from the ceiling light. "And why did the weather have to change today?" she grumbled, scooting a pair of discarded shoes toward the closet. "It couldn't stay nice one more day, could it? No, it has to be damp and cold. I bet he's expecting me to back out, to cancel, and then he can make some rude remark about wimpy women."

She rummaged through a back corner of her closet, emerging with a triumphant shout that caused Rocky's ears to lift up. "Perfect!" She dropped the heavy sweatshirt with the Colorado mountains emblazoned on the front over the turtleneck she had already put on and straightened the two sets of sleeves.

Bending over, she buckled thick hiking boots around her

ankles and petted Rocky's head. "What do you think?" she asked, standing up. "Fashion statement or what?"

The sweatshirt, long underwear, and warm corduroy jeans disguised most of her figure, but at least she wouldn't be cold. After securing Rocky in his pen, she picked up the backpack she had loaded with a thermos of hot chocolate, fresh baked cookies, and apples and slipped it over one shoulder. "Watch the house, boy," she instructed Rocky, snagging a rain jacket before she left.

Jake was waiting in the high school parking lot when she arrived, his pickup parked near the cars the students would have left when they took the team van. He had the local newspaper open on the steering wheel in front of him, and he lowered it when she rapped on his window.

"Morning."

A few rays of sunshine sparkled on his windshield and reflected around them, banishing some of the gloom. His warm smile dispersed more of it. Her lips felt dry. She licked them quickly. "Hi. Did you find Mandy's house all right?"

He nodded. "Anna barely had time to say goodbye to me before she ran off. Something about seeing Jessie's new doll."

Christine laughed at his disgruntled frown and then felt disposed to give him some comfort. "That should last about five minutes. Jessie's not big into dolls either."

He brightened and folded up the paper, tossing it over his shoulder into the back seat. "Really? I was worried I was going to have to find the doll aisle at the store next time I went shopping."

He leaned over and unlocked the passenger door. "Ready?"

She hesitated, wondering if she should drive since she

had invited him. Why had she let Mandy talk her into this? She usually supported her brother's teams, but on a day like this, he would have expected her to stay home. What would he say when he saw her—and with a date?

Jake was still watching her. ''Yeah, just a minute.'' She ran back to her car and grabbed the backpack, pushing down the lock on the door before slamming it shut.

He had her door open before she could catch the handle. ''Did I need to pack a lunch or something?'' He pointed to the bag she had dropped at her feet.

''No, I just brought some snacks. Hot chocolate and some cookies I baked last night.'' She didn't add that she had baked them in the middle of the night because she couldn't sleep, thinking about being with him again.

''Great! I haven't had homebaked cookies since . . .'' He frowned in concentration and then smacked his forehead with one hand. ''Since the last batch you baked for me.''

She chuckled. ''Well, don't get used to it. I like baking, but I don't do it that often.''

''Come on, Christine,'' he wheedled, ''take pity on a poor bachelor. If not me, what about my sister?''

''If your sister has even an ounce of your charm, she'll do fine.''

The words slipped out before she could stop them. She stared at him, embarrassed. ''I didn't mean that the way it sounded, Jake.''

He grinned. ''Yes you did. You're still upset with me about the way I conned you into babysitting that first day.''

''You didn't really con me . . .'' She frowned at his profile. ''You did, didn't you?''

''I didn't think it would be so easy.''

He swung the car toward the line of cars at the edge of the golf course and parked behind them. Turning off the engine, he shifted until he was facing her. "I did give you a chance to suggest someone else first."

"And when I didn't, you moved in for the kill." She crossed her arms over her chest.

He bent forward and pressed a kiss against her lips. "Hey, I said thank you, didn't I?" he asked and then jumped out of the car.

Her body wouldn't move. The kiss, the easy humor, she couldn't think. When the door opened at her back, she turned around quickly and would have fallen out of the truck if he hadn't caught her.

He edged her onto the step, his hand secure around her arm. "Come on. You said they started at ten, didn't you?"

She nodded. How could he disconcert her so easily? Not even her brothers had been able to make her lose her power of speech before. And they had often tried.

"Wouldn't want to forget this." He picked up the backpack and led her down the path toward the small crowd gathered at the crest of the hill, his hand still tight around her arm.

The golf course was situated at the edge of town, a wide ring of trees around its perimeter. The association allowed the cross-country team to practice and race on its property as long as the young men and women stayed away from the greens. Luke and his assistant coach had easily marked a route that led the runners around the outer edges of the course for five kilometers.

They paused away from the others. From her position, she could see Luke talking with two men his age, their heads bent over a trio of clipboards. "Luke ran against the other two coaches during high school," she explained to Jake, glad to see her voice had returned, "and they like to get together and have their teams meet sometime during the season. Luke has one boy and one girl who could make it to state this year," she ended proudly.

"Really?" Jake leaned his elbows on the low fence that surrounded this part of the golf course. "I didn't realize any of the seniors were that strong."

"Actually, it's not the seniors that he's watching. Diana is a junior and Shawn is a sophomore. Shawn didn't want to try out for the team because he thought it would interfere with his studies. He just runs for exercise, he said. Luke had to do a lot of talking to convince him to join the team."

She pointed to several runners warming up, their purple and gold uniforms bright against the grey sky. "Diana is the tall brunette. And Shawn is over there, with the short blond hair."

Luke whistled and his team gathered around him while the others met with their coaches. Christine gave Jake tidbits of information about the local runners as they waited for the race to start. After a few minutes of pep talk, the teams each gave a shouted cheer and then the girls lined up at the starting line. "Watch the flags so you stay on the route," Luke told them. "Runners, take your mark, set, GO!"

At the sound of the starting gun, the runners were off. Christine leaned forward to see around the crowd and found her face pressed against Jake's shoulder. The rough edge of his leather coat rubbed against her cheek and she could smell the pine scent of his soap. "Where do they go?" he asked over the din of parents and friends urging them on.

"That way." She pointed toward the thick stand of trees separating them from the golf course proper. "They come out of the trees and stay on the edge of the fairways until they get back here."

"Come on." He grabbed her arm and ducked under the fence.

"What are you doing?" His grip was tight and she could barely talk as he raced her across the rough ground.

"You don't just stand there and wait for them to come back, do you?"

She usually did, visiting with friends or parents, or sitting in the car with a book. Her brother ran to various parts of the course, shouting encouragement and times to his team, but she considered that part of his job.

She didn't have enough breath to share any of this with Jake. He was tugging her along, steering her past fallen trees and over ruts in the ground. The parents had stopped their shouting, and she imagined some of them wandering back to their cars to sit in comfort until the first runner appeared out of the woods. The boys would be running in place or stretching, getting ready for their own turn on the course.

Jake slowed and looked around. "Where do we go now?"

She studied their surroundings. "I'm not sure." She had walked the path once when Luke was marking it, but they had been talking about his team and she hadn't been paying attention. Not that it mattered now. With the clouds darkening the woods, the normal landmarks were obscured.

A shout sounded from their left. "This way," he said.

He moved slower now, his head cocked as if he were listening for sounds. He slid his hand down until their fingers were entwined. They carefully picked their way over limbs and brush.

"How long before the first runner makes it to the finish line?" He held a branch back from her face and helped her climb over a log.

"Twenty-five minutes, maybe." She stepped around a stump and tried to ignore the currents running up and down her arm. Even with gloves separating their skin, she could feel heat. "Depends on the route. Luke tries to find the cleanest path, but he also likes his runners to get the full cross-country effect."

"Really?" He kicked a rock and she scooted closer to him when a small animal darted away. She hoped he didn't notice her lapse of good sense. "I thought it would take all day, that they'd run toward Kansas City, Joplin, you know, a real cross-country route."

She tugged on his arm until he stopped. "You did not." She peered into his face. The shadows hid his expression but she sensed he was grinning. "Come on, Jake, you've been to cross-country meets before."

"One or two." He reached over and plucked a leaf from her hair, watching it drift to the ground before he faced her again. "But not with you."

His arms encircled her, one hand at the small of her back and the other cupping her neck. She lifted her face. His mouth was cool from the autumn air. His hand gently kneaded her shoulders, drawing her closer.

She didn't know what sense nudged her to lift her head. Her eyes widened at a crashing sound to the right of them. She grabbed Jake around the arm, propelling them out of the way just as the runners came through the small opening that led back to the start of the course.

They tumbled to the ground and landed with Christine sprawled across his shins, her face on a pile of rotting twigs. She gingerly sat up and wiped a hand across her face, feeling for cuts or scrapes. Surprised to find none, she sent him a cautious look.

He lay on his back, one hand over his face. "I've never had anyone react to my kisses that way" he murmured.

"It wasn't your kiss." She stood up and dusted off her pants, shaking her foot until her boot righted itself.

"That makes me feel better."

She reached down and grabbed his hand. Her intent to help him up stopped when she found she would have better luck moving a mountain.

"Get up. They're headed back."

He moved his hand and peered at her through narrowed eyes. "What?"

"The runners. They've probably crossed the finish line by now."

He cautiously pushed himself to a sitting position. "You're not going to throw me into the bushes again, are you?"

She had a strong urge to do just that. "Get up and stop being so silly." She reached down and yanked him to his feet, relieved when he came up easily. She suspected he gave her a lot of help, but she didn't care. She felt safer when they were standing up. Not that it had mattered earlier.

She pushed away the thoughts. "Didn't you see the runners? Or hear them?"

"Is that what happened? I thought it was your kissing."

"I know when somebody's making fun of me." She swung around and headed back the way they had come. "I won't kiss you again."

"Oh, really?"

She had no warning. One minute she was walking down the path and the next, she was snug against his chest, his mouth covering hers.

He released her as quickly as he had grabbed her. "You won't?"

"I didn't kiss you," she said when she regained her breath. "You kissed me."

A dark glint shone in his eyes and she backed away, her hands up. "Jake, don't. The other runners should be coming through any minute."

"They'll be paying attention to where they're going," he growled, reaching for her.

She jumped nimbly out of his way and spun around. Her feet barely touched the ground as she raced over fallen limbs and logs. Jake crashed through the brush, his footsteps heavy behind her. Darting him one quick grin over her shoulder, she emerged from the brush just as Diana crossed the finish line.

Christine skidded to a stop near the fence and waited as the other runners appeared. She had lost track of time, but from Luke's excited expression, she knew he was pleased with Diana's performance. He was walking with her as she cooled down. He hoped the young woman would be able to run a time that would qualify her for the state meet. From meet from his reaction, Christine suspected Diana had exceeded his expectations.

"So, it's over?" Jake asked. He stood next to her, his hands in his pockets, and stamped his feet to ward off the cold.

Her neck hunched into her sweatshirt, she shook her head, wishing she hadn't left her rain jacket in the car when she grabbed her backpack. Her ears were freezing. The jacket wasn't much protection against the cold, but it did have a hood. "Not yet. The boys have to run now." She gestured toward the group of young men running in place, their breath fanning around their faces in white puffs of air.

"So, another twenty minutes in the woods?"

His suggestive voice was low. They were standing several feet away from the other spectators, but she glanced around nervously anyway. Her ears weren't turning red just from the cold. "Stop it, Jake!" she hissed.

"What? I just mentioned the woods."

"I know what you were saying." She turned her back on him and focused on the boys lining up by the coaches. Luke had raised his arm and even though she couldn't hear him, she knew he was giving last minute instructions.

A blast of arctic air found its way down her neck and she shivered. When a jacket appeared around her shoulders, she jolted. "Didn't you check the weather forecast?" Jake growled, tugging the thick collar around her ears. "Maybe I should take you back in the woods, just to warm you up."

She burrowed into the warmth of the coat, inhaling his scent as she did so. "I had another jacket in my car," she mumbled through the thick fabric of the collar. The heavy corduroy felt heavenly around her ears. "We could have some hot chocolate. And thanks," she added belatedly, wondering if she should refuse the jacket. Now that he had taken off the coat, she could see that he only wore a heavy flannel shirt over a thick woolen sweater.

He untwisted the lid of the thermos and poured a generous helping of the dark liquid into it. "Here."

Before she could move her hands from the pockets, he had the makeshift cup at her lips. She sipped the hot drink gratefully, her eyes watching him over the rim. His eyes were almost the same color as the chocolate, she noticed, letting the heat of his glance and the drink slide into her system. From somewhere behind her, she heard shouts and cheers, but she couldn't tear her gaze away from his.

"Mind if I have some?" he asked after he lowered the cup.

She nodded, her voice trapped somewhere within her throat. She watched as he carefully turned the cup until he was drinking from the same side she had used. The action seemed more intimate than any she had ever shared with a man and her heart stuttered inside the layers of clothes she was wearing.

He emptied the leftover drops on the ground before securing the lid back on the thermos. "Now what?"

A cheer sounded from behind her and she slowly turned her head toward the group gathering at the finish line. Shawn ran across first, his face lighting up as Luke congratulated him with the same enthusiasm he had earlier shown Diana.

She was amazed so much time had passed. "The boys are coming in. In a few minutes, they'll tally the results and give out the medals," she said.

"What?"

She glanced over her shoulder. Jake was watching her with a frown on his face. "The race is almost over. When everyone comes in, they'll announce the final results."

"The race."

He sounded exasperated. Looking at his set face, she opened her mouth and then snapped it shut, biting back the other details about the end of the race that she had been about to share with him.

He hadn't been asking her about the race. She clenched her fists. What did he expect from her? One moment, he was bragging about how he had charmed her into babysitting, and the next, he was causing her to forget her own name with his kisses. A woman could easily lose her footing trying to keep up with him.

"We'll be giving out the medals in just a few minutes," Luke announced before she had a chance to say anything. "If you'll gather over here please."

She gave a sigh of relief, glad someone else had taken the choice away from her. It would give rise to comments if she and Jake continued to linger at the edges of the crowd, especially since Luke had called them together and most of the people watching the meet knew she was the coach's sister. Her hands tucked into Jake's coat pockets, she stepped up to the group without waiting to see if he would follow her.

If he decided to leave, she could always hitch a ride with Luke. He might tease her about her choice of escorts, but he would at least get her back to her car safely. She patted the jacket against her jeans, feeling for the security of her car keys.

No satisfying lump met her probing fingers. She slipped her hand out of the coat pocket and shoved it into her jeans pocket. No keys. She patted the other pocket but heard only the jingle of a few loose coins.

Closing her eyes, she tried to remember what she had done when she arrived at the parking lot. She had been surprised to see Jake already there, assuming that he tended to run behind in all of his activities. Seeing his truck parked in the lot had given her a jolt. She had jumped out of the car and hurried to his side, tapping on his window to get his attention.

She opened her eyes and groaned. When he had offered to drive, she had run to the car and grabbed the backpack without reaching into the ignition to get her keys. Another groan slipped over her lips as she recalled how she had automatically pushed the lock down on the door before shutting it.

Her brother would never let her live this down. Whatever she did, she had to return with Jake. She would have to swallow her pride and ask him to drive her home so she could get the spare set of keys out of her dresser. It would only be a matter of moments to find the house key she kept hidden in the back flower garden.

She took a step backward, intent on finding Jake and convincing him to wait for the award ceremony. She bumped into a solid figure and felt his hands slide around her waist. ''Yes?'' he drawled against her cheek.

Her breathing faltered. ''I just—'' she swallowed and started again. ''I just wanted to make sure you hadn't left yet.''

''And leave you here?'' He slid around to her side, one arm still around her waist. ''How would that look?''

She shrugged, trying to ignore the tiny prick of hurt that lodged itself in her. So he didn't want the others to think he was a chump? Wasn't that why she didn't want to go back with Luke? The ribbing that would follow would be hard to take. She'd rather deal with Jake than have to endure her brother's comments for the next millennium.

They stood side by side, Jake's arm loose around her waist, as the winners were announced. As expected, Shawn had easily outdistanced the other young men and he gave a shy grin when Luke handed him the first place medal. Diana smiled at her parents and her little sister quickly joined her, holding the medal up with a proud smile of her own.

''She'll be a runner herself,'' Jake said with a knowing jerk of his head toward Diana's little sister.

''You think so?'' She studied the girl. Her legs were long and slender and she moved with the frisky grace of a colt.

Her dark hair swung behind her in a thick ponytail, completing the picture of a healthy young animal.

"I've seen them running together on the weekends, past one of the job sites," he explained. "One of these days, she'll give her sister a run for her money."

"You knew about the runners," she stated, wondering how foolish she had sounded when she was telling him about the team. She should have realized that in a town the size of Durant, most people would be aware of the local talent. And since he had once been the local talent and was still considered one by many of the inhabitants, he would be more attuned than most people.

"Not everything. You had some insights from your brother I didn't know."

They headed toward the parked cars, their arms bumping against each other several times as they negotiated the rough terrain. Luke had been talking with the other coaches so she had decided to call him later with congratulations. Right now, she just wanted to get home and away from Jake and the conflicting emotions he raised in her.

"Hey, Chris, wait up!" Her brother's shout halted her a few feet from Jake's truck.

Luke's long stride caught up with them quickly. "So, what did you think?" he asked with a proud grin on his face.

She hugged him around the shoulders. "They were great, Luke."

"Did you see Diana? If she keeps up that pace, she'll qualify for state without any trouble." He leaned against a tree and crossed his arms over his chest, watching them with a curious light in his eyes. "Haven't seen you around much, Jake. Keeping busy, I hear."

"Can't complain." Jake had shifted away from her and

had his arms crossed over his chest, his legs braced apart as if he were prepared for battle.

She might have found the situation amusing if she weren't the woman caught in the middle. Luke's questioning glance and Jake's defensive stance clearly stated that they were sizing each other up. *Just as if I was a prize they were protecting,* she thought.

She nudged Luke's foot with her boot. "You going to be around for Thanksgiving?"

"Hmm?" His gaze slid away from Jake's and back to her. "What? Thanksgiving? Sure. We'll be done with the season by then." His eyes narrowed and he swung his attention back to Jake before returning to her face. "What about you?"

She wished she hadn't brought up the topic. She had only thought about directing Luke's attention away from Jake and back to her. Once the question left her mouth, she had realized it wasn't polite to discuss personal plans in front of a guest. And whether she had driven or not, Jake was her guest. Thanks to Mandy's meddling, she had invited him to the meet and had nothing to show for it except her bruised pride.

And a warm coat. Even with him standing there scowling at her brother, she couldn't ignore the way he had wrapped his coat around her, sacrificing his comfort for hers. She snuggled into its protective warmth. His scent rose around her, blocking out the sharp odor of the autumn woods. A clean masculine scent that reminded her of the way he looked when he came in from his construction sites, his boots muddy, his jeans grimy from crawling around unfinished rooms, his eyes alight with excitement.

Her attention shifted toward the temporary course. The cross-country teams had picked up their bags and were heading toward the vans, the runners chatting together as if they hadn't just run against each other. She knew that some of the runners were related, living in different towns during the school year and gathering at a common grand-parent's house for holidays or summer activities. Her own family boasted relatives in at least three of the surrounding communities, even though none of them were closely re-lated. Her grandparents had retired to Florida three years earlier, and her aunts and uncles were scattered throughout other parts of the country.

She wondered about Jake's family. His parents were both dead, but she didn't know about any other relatives. Would he be celebrating Thanksgiving alone with Anna? Or had Marilyn already proffered an invitation?

"I'll check with Mom," she heard Luke say, "but she won't mind. She always makes enough for a small army. Dad's great about gathering in strays of his own."

Jake's laugh rumbled through the woods and she saw three of the girls turn their heads to look at him. "Are you calling me a stray?"

Luke's closed fist reached out and lightly punched Jake's arm just below the shoulder. "If you want some of the best home cooking you'll ever taste, you'll be happy to be a stray."

"If it's anything like Christine's . . ." He grinned at her and she flushed at the compliment she read in his eyes.

"Where do you think she learned?" Luke pushed him-self away from the tree and turned toward the vans. "Thanks for coming, sis." He gave her a tight hug and a quick smack on the forehead. "I didn't think you'd come out on a day like today. You notice Seth stayed away."

"Well—" She didn't know what to say. He had all but

advertised that normally she would have stayed home in bad weather.

"I'm glad she didn't," Jake put in. He fell into step with Luke, leaving Christine to follow behind them. "That Diana is something else. How does she match up with the other runners in the state?"

A few steps behind them, she listened as they discussed Durant's chances at the state meet. She wasn't surprised when their talk veered toward the other high school sports, and she bit back a grin when she heard them agreeing about the referee calls at the last football game that had "lost the game for them."

"Why don't you ref?" she asked Jake as he opened the pickup door for her. She handed him his coat before getting in and then huddled into her sweatshirt, trying to ignore the bereft feeling that stole over her.

"Are you kidding? That has got to be the most thankless job in the world."

"Yeah, but you know so much about the sport." She turned toward him and bumped her backpack with her foot. "Oh, you didn't have any cookies."

By the time she had the package open, they were at the edge of town. The high school was to the left and her house was to the right. For a fleeting moment, she thought about letting him drop her off at her car. Her friend, Abby, lived across from the school and she could drive her home for her keys.

But she couldn't imagine Jake leaving her without making sure her car would start. Taking a deep breath, she handed him a cookie and then blurted out, "Would you mind taking me home first? I locked my keys in the car."

"What?"

"I was planning to drive us," she explained quickly.

"When you offered, I just grabbed the backpack and locked the car without thinking. My keys are still in the ignition."

"Oh, yeah?" He swung toward the parking lot of the high school, munching on a cookie.

"I have a spare set of keys at home," she said, wondering if maybe she had misjudged him. Was he just going to leave her in the parking lot and let her fend for herself? Not that she couldn't, she reminded herself.

"Let's see what we can do first." He pulled in next to her small car and reached under the seat, picking up a small black box before opening his door.

She hopped out and followed him over to her car. He was squatting next to the driver's door, his now ungloved fingers lightly tracing over the lock. "What are you doing?" she asked.

"You wouldn't believe how many times some joker has locked us out of a truck or building. I was paying a fortune to locksmiths before I decided to learn how to do it myself."

Over his shoulder, she watched him take out several small tools and jiggle them in the lock for several minutes before she heard the button pop up. He pulled the handle and the door swung open. "Your chariot, my lady," he said with an exaggerated bow before carefully replacing his tools.

"I'm impressed." She reached in and plucked her keys from the ignition. "So if your building work ever fails . . ."

"I have another trade to rely on," he finished. He leaned one hand on the roof of her car, trapping her between the open door and his body. "I meant what I told your brother, Christine. Thanks for inviting me."

"You're welcome." She couldn't lift her head. If she

did, her lips would be only inches away from him and she didn't want him to think she was asking for another kiss.

She didn't have time to worry about it. He lifted her chin with one finger and tipped her head until their mouths were aligned. The kiss was gentle.

"If I don't see you before," he murmured, raising his head from hers, "I'll see you at Thanksgiving."

He was at the door of his truck before her senses returned. "What did you say?"

"I'll see you at Thanksgiving," he called over the bed of his truck. "Your brother invited us."

Christine sank into her seat and closed the door. Aware that he was waiting for her to start her car, she turned the key and then gave him a quick wave before driving toward her part of town, her mind mulling over his last comment.

Thanksgiving with Jake. A whole afternoon with him. They could visit, relax, nibble on her mother's appetizers before dinner . . .

She shuddered, coming back to reality with a thud. Her brothers would be there, too. Luke's attitude was mild compared to the interrogation Seth would give him. And she didn't want to consider what her mom and dad would think. Her mother wanted grandchildren. She wouldn't be rude or even say anything to Jake, but she would watch him with a hopeful smile on her face, one that had worried enough dates that Christine had quit bringing them home.

And now Luke had invited one for her. She could pretend that Jake was only there because of Luke, but she knew it would take little for her family to see that he meant something to her. Her lips still tingled from his last kiss. Somehow, before Thanksgiving, she had to convince him to decline the invitation, find him another place to go, or come down with a horrendous case of the flu.

Chapter Seven

Two weeks before Thanksgiving, the first winter storm hit the area. The people of Durant didn't mind winter, even embraced the snows when they came, but this storm surprised them, coming after a period of balmy weather warm enough to keep windows and doors open. After the cross-country meet, the clouds had blown away and temperatures had ranged in the 60's and 70's for the next two weeks, encouraging people to put away their winter coats and pull on a pair of shorts.

Christine dug through her front closet to find her heavy coat and then through her other jackets to find a pair of gloves. By the time she was dressed for the weather, she knew she would be late to work. The trip that usually took only a few minutes would be slow going with slippery roads. At least the route from Main Street to the hospital would be clear. She kept reminding herself of that as she inched down the side streets.

The snow plow was scraping and spreading cinders when she slowed for her final turn. She raised a gloved hand toward the driver and then carefully eased into the intersection, breathing a sigh of relief when she drove onto the cleared road. She had grown up learning to drive on snowy roads, but each year she had to remember the rules all over again.

"Winter came in with a vengeance," she announced to Ethel as she crossed the lobby. She tugged off her gloves and stuffed them into her coat pockets, not surprised to see that the older woman had made it in to her volunteer post. Like the postal service, not much could keep Ethel from her appointed rounds.

"Technically, it's not even winter yet." Ethel smiled from her location behind the information desk. "December 21st is the first day of winter."

"Then what is that outside?" Christine leaned her elbows on the counter and grinned at her older friend.

"An appetizer?"

Laughing, Christine straightened and headed for the stairs. She was already late, and the few moments she would save using the elevator wouldn't matter as much as having the exercise. She flexed her fingers on the way up, trying to regain their normal shape after clenching them on the steering wheel.

"I'm glad to see you." Angela, the nurse on duty, gave her a relieved smile when Christine arrived at the station. "Beth and Kelly both called and said they wouldn't be able to make it in until their roads are cleared. The wind really picked up last night and they have drifts several feet high on the back roads."

"The plows were still working on Main Street," Christine said. "It could be afternoon before the other roads are open."

"Maybe the rest of town will stay inside and we won't have much business."

"We can only hope."

The morning passed in routine work, helping the handful of patients on the floor with their morning rituals, checking their vitals, refilling supply closets, adding data to the new computer system that had recently been installed. Listening to the radio while she typed in patient information, Christine heard that the schools had been closed for the day. She idly wondered what Jake and Anna were doing.

A few visitors ventured in after lunch. They stopped at the nurse's station to give a weather update or just for a quick chat before heading to the rooms. A retired high school teacher was being treated for heart problems and several friends had taken advantage of the school closing to visit. Christine found three of them laughing with Mrs. Peabody when she entered the room with her former science teacher's medication.

"Now, here's a success story." The silver-haired woman scooted up in her bed and accepted the cup of water and pill with a smile.

"Me?" Christine glanced at the others, recognizing one of her English teachers and a math teacher. The other occupant had never been a teacher, but as one of the descendants of the town's founding fathers, Mary Fletcher didn't let much happen in town before she was involved.

Mrs. Peabody gulped down the pill and gave a delicate shudder before handing the empty cup to Christine. "I do hate swallowing pills."

"Something we all have to do," Christine couldn't resist saying.

When the women laughed, she received the response she had expected. Mrs. Peabody had been notorious for pushing her students, requiring them to give their best each day of the year. When someone would complain about homework, she would fix them with a stern stare over her glasses and recite, "Something we all have to do." Christine had never been exactly sure what it meant, but she had always finished her homework on time.

"Touché! Didn't I say she was a success?" Mrs. Peabody gave the others a broad smile.

"I'd say we have quite a few success stories," Mrs. Baker, the math teacher, said with a friendly look at Christine. "All the Hunter children have turned out well and Mandy Sandus is doing a wonderful job with the kindergarten class."

They named others who had passed through their classes, encompassing many of the business owners in town, the minister of the local church, and the hospital administrator.

"Don't forget Jake Reynolds," Mrs. Shields put in.

"Of course not." Mrs. Baker smiled at her friends. "Andrew just loves his new house. We're spending Thanksgiving there this year."

Mrs. Baker's son had graduated several years before Christine, in the same class as her brother Seth, and now sold insurance. She knew he had recently commissioned a house from Jake, moving in during the summer. As one of his clients and a friend, she had been invited to the house-warming barbecue and gone with her brother. She had been impressed with the house and understood his mother's pride.

"I hear Jake and his sister are joining your family for Thanksgiving this year," Mrs. Fletcher said with an openly curious look on her face. "Your mother mentioned it when I met her at the store yesterday."

Christine felt the color rush up her neck and she busied

herself fluffing Mrs. Peabody's pillows and straightening the sheets. "Luke invited him."

From the corner of her eye, she saw the women exchange glances. Why did Luke have to do this to her? And since when did her mother give their social calendar to Mary Fletcher? Didn't she realize that was as good as taking out an ad in the paper?

She hadn't even seen Jake since the cross-country meet. With the bout of warm weather, she assumed he would be using every moment of daylight to finish what he could before winter set in, but surely he could have given her a call in the evening.

Why would he do that? she asked herself, unable to meet the eyes of the teachers she had studied under only a few years earlier. She had been a good student and she was a capable nurse, but she still found herself quavering when she saw one of them, wondering for a moment if she had forgotten her homework before she remembered that she was an adult. With all of them watching her now, she almost felt as if she should confess she had shared a few kisses with Jake.

She shook off the feeling and summoned up her brisk nursing attitude. This was her domain. "Fifteen more minutes and then Mrs. Peabody needs her rest," she informed the group.

"Oh, come now, I'm sure you could stretch the time a little bit, considering . . ." Mrs. Baker said, her lips curved upward in what Christine would have called a wheedling smile in anyone else.

"Sorry."

She hurried out of the room before they could say anything else and leaned against the wall, her hands pressed at her side. What was the matter with her? A few comments about Jake and she was ready to collapse on the floor. While she had followed his football career with the rest of the town, she barely knew the man he had become.

Which didn't matter. She knew enough to know that she wanted to find out more about him. His devil-may-care attitude intrigued her, combined as it was with his genuine concern for his sister. His business reputation was rock solid and people all over town talked about his ability to finish a job in record time with satisfying results. He didn't require his crews to work hours any different than his own and often let them go home hours before he did.

"Christine?"

She lifted her head and met Angela's interested gaze. "Are you okay?"

Christine pushed away from the wall and ran her hands down the side of her uniform. "I'm fine." She glanced over her shoulder at the room she had just left. "Would you be sure to clear out Mrs. Peabody's room in about fifteen minutes? She needs her rest."

Angela nodded. "Dr. Sanders was by a few minutes ago. He wondered if you could stop by his office before you leave."

She nodded. Since his marriage to Mandy, their relationship had undergone a subtle shift. He was still the doctor and she was still the nurse, but he sometimes asked for her opinion on situations in town that she would understand more than he did, being the relative newcomer. When they weren't on duty, they enjoyed social time together. She and Mandy had been best friends since kindergarten, and while she had survived when Mandy moved to the city, she was thrilled to have her back.

She stayed beyond her regular departure time that night, waiting for her replacement to make it into town. The sun had melted some of the snow on the roads, making travel easier. Looking out the window across from the nurse's station, she saw that the town glittered brightly under the new fallen snow. By tomorrow, she knew, the leftover snow would begin to collect road dirt and become grey, but for now, she enjoyed the pristine white that covered the fallen leaves and dead branches that littered the yards surrounding the hospital.

By the time she finished going over the charts with the night nurse, she was sure Greg would have gone home. Mandy and Jesse would have been home for the day, and she imagined her friend would have found the day challenging. She often stated that it was easier to keep a classroom of kindergartners occupied for a day than to find ways to entertain one first grader.

Christine wasn't sure she would agree. The few times that she had been with Anna since the cross-country meet went by all too quickly. Reading, make-believe, baking. . . . Before she knew it, the time was up, Jake was home, and she had no reason to stay.

Especially since he hadn't asked her out. She didn't want to dwell on why he didn't, but she couldn't help sighing as she tapped on Greg's door.

She pushed it open when he called a gruff, "Come in."

"What are you doing here? I thought you'd be gone by now." She perched on the edge of a chair and popped one of the mints he kept on his desk into her mouth.

"I planned to be. I was waiting for some reports and they just came in." He scribbled a few more notes on a tablet and then leaned back in his chair, his hands cupped behind his head. "How are you, Christine?"

"Fine. Why?"

"No real reason. I just like to know how the nurses are doing."

"We're fine. We could use a few more on staff," she stated, deciding to take advantage of this opportunity. "Our shifts tend to be pretty close together."

"I know. I've already talked to the board and we'll be running some advertisements in the next few weeks."

He dropped his chair back on the floor and propped his elbows on the desk. "What about you? You're still satisfied with your job here?"

She gave him a wary look. "Yes, it's what I've always wanted to do. Is there some problem with my work, Greg?" She leaned forward, wondering if he was trying to gently tell her that they had decided to let someone else be head nurse.

"No, of course not. You're one of the most competent nurses I've ever worked with." He tipped his head to one side. "It's nothing I can pinpoint, Christine, but I just have this feeling. . . . Is something going on?"

She studied him for a moment. When he had first arrived in Durant, he had caused a lot of talk among the nurses and other unattached women in town, each one hoping they could be the next Mrs. Sanders. Christine had not been among them, more concerned about her recent promotion to head nurse. He had been tough on her and the others, but she knew now that he was no tougher on them than he was on himself. Medicine was more than a job to him and his concern for his patients was genuine.

He was watching her with the same gentle air he used when listening to a patient. She sighed and crossed her legs, linking her hands over her knee. She could use some advice. Rocky was a good sounding board, but it would be nice to talk to someone who would answer back. "I don't know, Greg. I just feel at loose ends. I like my work,'' she said quickly, ''and I can't imagine not nursing. But sometimes . . .''

''You wonder where your life is headed?''

She nodded. He had summed up her restless feelings perfectly. ''Lately, I've been wondering what I'm going to do.'' She didn't add that the feelings had only intensified since her encounter with Jake.

''Have you ever been anywhere besides Durant?'' he asked.

''Not really.'' She thought for a moment and then shook her head. ''We went to Chicago when I was little for a family wedding and we made regular trips to Kansas City. Other than those trips and my years at college, I've never been anywhere.''

''Maybe you need to get away, see what's outside Missouri. It helped Amanda to go off for a while.''

She knew her friend's few years in Kansas City had convinced her that she belonged in the small town. ''There's no place like home,'' she said softly, echoing Dorothy's discovery after her trip to Oz.

Greg grinned. ''Something like that. Of course, Christine, home isn't just a place.'' He tapped his chest. ''It's more a sense of belonging. I've lived in several different places and I could probably live in any one of them again. If Amanda and Jessie are with me,'' he stated emphatically.

She nodded. Family was important to her, too. Her years at college had been difficult, even though she had come home most weekends and spent her holidays with her family. She had gone to classes during the summer, cramming four years of study into three. When she finally received her diploma and moved back to Durant, she had been excited about returning and hadn't even considered taking a job somewhere else.

So why was she so restless now? Was Jake right? Was she cautious, afraid to take risks? Was that why she had never left Durant?

She refused to consider that possibility. Being tied to a community because of loyalty was nothing to be ashamed of. She smiled at Greg. "Maybe I just need a vacation. As soon as you hire some new nurses, I'll take a week or two. That's probably all I need, just some time to clear the cobwebs from my head."

They visited a few more minutes, talking about their plans for the Thanksgiving weekend. His ex-wife had called to say that she wouldn't be able to have Jessie visit this year, since she would be attending meetings with her husband in Europe. Rather than devastating Jessie, she had been thrilled about having Thanksgiving with her father and her new family. "Rebecca said she's going to just relax and watch us cook," he said with a chuckle. "I'll believe it when I see it."

"Oh, you'll see it," Christine said, getting to her feet. "Rebecca came to our house a couple of years ago when Mandy couldn't get off, and she didn't raise a finger. Except to eat, of course."

They laughed and he held the door for her. Clicking off the light, he followed her down the hallway and toward the back door the doctors and nurses used to get to the parking lot. He draped an arm companionably over her shoulders. "Listen, I'll see what I can do about getting you some time off. As my mom used to say, you only get one chance through life. And don't hesitate to come by if you just need to visit."

"Thanks, Greg." On impulse, she leaned over and kissed his cheek. "Mandy's pretty lucky."

He gave her a wide grin. "I remind her of that all the time."

Laughing, she waved and headed toward her car at the end of the parking lot. Her steps slowed when she saw the tall figure lounging against the hood. A pulsing started at the base of her neck.

"Hi." She fumbled in her purse for her keys, the thick gloves hampering her efforts.

"Who was that?" Jake jerked his head toward the direction she had come, a scowl on his face.

She glanced over her shoulder. The building shadowed the edge of the parking lot and she could barely make out Greg bending to unlock his own car. "Greg?" she asked, her brows raised in puzzlement as she turned back to Jake.

"That was Greg Sanders?" He peered into the gloom created by the hovering clouds and then turned back to her. "You were kissing Greg Sanders?"

She succeeded in finding her keys and pulled them out. She reached forward and nudged him out of her way, sliding the key into the lock. "He gave me some advice and I was thanking him."

"Oh, I see."

"What is the matter with you?" The lock popped up and she released the key, stepping back so she could see his face more clearly. He looked tired and she almost reached forward to smooth her fingers over the ridges along his face. It took all her willpower to keep her hands at her sides. "Did you come over here to complain about what I do after hours?"

"I came over here to see if you were free this evening," he snapped.

"Oh." A tiny flutter started in the base of her stomach and worked its way up. "I, well, I . . ." She swallowed, knowing she sounded as flustered as she felt.

"I stayed home with Anna today and I could do with some adult company. I thought, maybe, we could rent a movie—something that isn't animated—and get some Chinese."

His invitation was going a long way toward erasing those restless feelings she had mentioned to Greg. She didn't want to consider what that meant. After two weeks of not seeing him or hearing from him, she just wanted to enjoy the moment of being with him, of knowing that he had sought her out.

"That sounds fun," she said tentatively, unwilling to let him know how much she wanted to be with him.

Greg drove past, honking at them, and Christine waved. She didn't even care if he reported to Mandy that she was standing in the parking lot talking to Jake.

"She should go to bed early," he was saying. "We went sledding and she's worn out. I thought we could eat dinner together and watch the movie after she goes to bed."

Her pleasure at the prospect of an evening alone with him dissolved. Anna. His sister would be with them. She liked Anna, even suspected her feelings were growing stronger for the little girl, but just once, she would like him to attempt to see her alone.

Why should he? she scolded herself. *You've shown that you're more than willing to take them as a package deal. The only time you haven't been with the two of them, you made the arrangements.*

"You know what, Jake, I'm busy after all. I just remembered." She reached for the handle and pulled it up partway before his hand caught her wrist, stopping her actions.

"What did I say?"

She stared at him. He really didn't understand. "Nothing, it's me." She closed her fingers over the handle again. "If you don't mind, I'd like to go home. It's been a long day."

His fingers tightened around her wrist. "I do mind." He tugged her hand until she released the door and pulled her around until she was facing him. "Are you mad because I haven't called you since the day of the meet?"

"No." Hurt, maybe, but they had no commitment. They'd shared a few kisses, that was all.

"I tried, at least twice," he said as if she hadn't spoken. "With this lull in the weather, we've been able to complete almost every project except for the interior work. It couldn't have come at a better time."

"I'm happy for you." She was glad, to an extent. No doubt, though, his calls had been to find someone to watch Anna so he could put in more hours. She hoped he didn't catch the bitter note in her voice.

"Anna's been a real trooper. She's gone to the after-school program most of the time and Mandy watched her last weekend for me. That's why I felt like I had to take today off for her. I just didn't know I'd be so tired after spending the day with her."

"Then maybe you should just call it a night, too," she said, trying to ease her hand away from his tight grip.

"Come on, Christine, I'm offering you dinner and a movie," he asked, his thumb sliding under the cuff of her jacket and gently rubbing against her skin. "Do you have a better offer?"

She had no defenses against his soft voice or the gentle assault on her skin. If she went home, she would enjoy a solitary meal with only Rocky for company. She could finish a book she had started over the weekend but the story would wait for her.

"No, I don't," she finally said. From the moment he'd tendered the invitation, she'd known she wouldn't be able to refuse. "I do need to take care of Rocky, though."

"That's fine." Now that she had agreed, he grinned at her. As if he really wants me to come over, she thought in bemusement. "I'll go look for a movie and order dinner. Mrs. Anderson is watching Anna until I get back."

He opened the door for her and held it until she had buckled her seatbelt. "See you in a little bit," he said. "And drive carefully. They've cleared most of the roads, but they'll still be slick."

"So, Rocky, what does this mean?" she asked the puppy as she pulled a blue sweater embroidered with snowmen over her head. Her curls sprang free of the turtleneck collar and she fluffed them up with her fingers. "He was upset when he saw me kissing Greg, only he didn't know it was Greg. He was almost rude when he invited me over. So, is he jealous, or is he just afraid I won't be around to help with Anna?"

She bent down and nuzzled Rocky under the chin. The puppy was starting to grow into his feet and ears and the top of his head reached her knees. He still stayed behind the gate, but she knew it was only a matter of time before he realized how easily he could jump over it.

Her brother had once suggested she put a door on the pantry so that it would be separated from the kitchen. Latching the gate, she eyed the arched opening. It wouldn't be hard to put in a door but it would be beyond her capabilities.

Jake. Now that the weather had changed, he would be

looking for inside work. She didn't know how much was left on the contracts he already had, but surely he could spare a few hours to help her. "Not that he really owes me," she explained to Rocky, patting him on his head, "but it would be a nice gesture."

She dug a tape measure out of her catch-all drawer and wrote down the measurements. Even without the figures, she knew a regular rectangular door wouldn't work. Before Rocky, she had hung a curtain over the opening, sewing one out of a brightly colored sheet that echoed the patterns in the living room and hooking it up from the inside of the pantry. Once she had found the need to keep the puppy locked up while she was gone, she had folded the sheet and tucked it away. Rocky's sharp little teeth would have shredded the material in just minutes.

Satisfied she had something to discuss with him when she arrived, she made her way to his house. The streets had been scraped clean but the melting snow had started to freeze with the cooler temperatures of the evening. Street-lights sparkled on the snow that covered the yards, glittering silvery white in the blue-grey of dusk. Lights shone in the homes she passed and smoke filtered out of the chimneys and into the sky. She could imagine people cozily tucked inside. The hustle and bustle of everyday life slowed down when the roads became impassable.

Jake's front porch light shone in invitation and she pulled into the driveway. Her boots crunched on the snow as she crossed the driveway to the back door. She had barely knocked when the door was yanked open.

"Hi, Christine!" Anna beamed at her and Christine couldn't help smiling back.

"Hi. I heard you had a busy day today." She stepped into the kitchen and unbuckled her boots, lining them up on the newspaper next to Jake's and Anna's. Melting snow plopped on the paper.

"Yeah, we went sledding. I fell off once but Jake caught me before I hit a tree."

"Thank you, Anna," Jake said dryly, coming into the room. He gave Christine a wry grin. "She was not in that much danger. The tree was at least ten feet away."

"But I could have slid into it," Anna argued.

"Sledding can be dangerous," Christine murmured, wondering which one was telling her the truth.

Anna gave her brother an "I told you so" smirk and he swatted a dish towel toward her bottom. She shrieked and giggled and raced into the living room before he could catch her again.

"She doesn't need any more encouragement," he muttered.

Christine laughed. His relationship with Anna reminded her of the teasing that existed between her brothers and her and yet it carried something more. Another level, almost like that of a parent to child.

"We usually have several broken bones after a snow day," she explained. "I don't know why we didn't today."

"Maybe because a number of parents were on The Hill today."

She pursed her lips together, considering his reasoning. Several small hills were good for sledding but the undisputed king was a hill near the middle of town, known simply as The Hill. She remembered sledding down The Hill many times during her teenage years. Most of the area was open and, after a heavy snowstorm like the one they had just experienced, was ideal for sleds of all sizes. A few more adventurous souls liked to sled around the trees that edged the area.

"You could be right," she said. "It would be great if we could help them understand how dangerous it is to sled by the trees."

"Did you ever consider the danger?"

He had moved several steps closer and she found it difficult to breathe. "I always used the middle paths," she said slowly.

"Always?"

She nodded, unable to pull her gaze away from him. She felt as if she had moved away from the safe, secure middle ground to a more dangerous place, a place where she could lose her footing. A place that promised a rush of excitement she had never experienced before.

He leaned toward her and his mouth covered hers, his lips traveling over hers with a tenderness she wouldn't have expected from him. Her hands snaked up his arms to curl around his shoulders as she tried to keep her balance. Her heartbeat slowed and then sped up.

She tried to remember why she hadn't wanted to come over, why she had fought so hard against her own desires. This is what she wanted, she told herself, holding on to him, feeling the play of his muscles under her fingers, the strength of his arms around her waist. What she needed.

He lifted his head and lightly flicked a finger over her lips. "Hello," he murmured.

"Hello," she echoed shyly. Her unabashed response to his kiss surprised and embarrassed her.

"We should probably get supper on the table before Anna comes back in." He turned away from her and picked up a stack of paper plates from the counter.

She studied his back for a moment, wondering if she had imagined the spark that had leapt between them. How could he act so nonchalant? Or did he greet everyone who came to his house for dinner with a kiss?

She almost choked on the image. She quickly pressed a hand against her mouth, shifting to one side when he moved toward the table with a load of dishes. Some people might welcome friends and acquaintances that way, but she couldn't see Jake Reynolds, construction boss and former football star, handing out kisses like they were candy.

So what did his kisses mean? Was she the only one who received them? Or was she one in a select group of women that he kissed?

She didn't have much time to ponder. "Would you fill those with water and ice?" he asked, pointing to three glasses sitting on the counter.

By the time she finished, he had set the table. "Anna!" he called.

She raced into the kitchen and plopped into a chair. "Did you wash up?" he asked.

She studied her hands. "They're not dirty."

"Wash." He pointed toward the sink and she climbed out of her chair, stomping toward the sink with dirty looks aimed at his back.

Christine bit down a grin, not wanting Anna to transfer her irritation to her. She knew the little girl's moods were mercurial and would shift quickly, but she knew she was in no shape to handle them. She was still reeling from the effects of Jake's kiss.

As soon as they finished grace, Anna knelt on a chair and reached across her plate for the rice, almost bumping over Christine's water glass in the process.

"Anna, remember your manners," Jake said. He handed Christine a box and she quietly thanked him before spooning cashew chicken onto her plate.

"But I'm starving," Anna said in a melodramatic voice.

Jake caught Christine's eye and grinned. Her hand froze halfway above her plate, dismayed by the yearnings that one glance had created in her.

She wanted to share glances like that with him often. She wanted to come home from work and fix dinner for him or have him bring supper home on his way back from a job site. She wanted to know that he reserved his kisses for her and for her alone.

She wanted him to love her as much as she feared she was beginning to love him.

Chapter Eight

She didn't know how she would make it through the rest of the evening. As long as Anna was up, she provided a buffer. Christine welcomed the little girl's chatter. She questioned Jake about the door in the pantry and calmly accepted his offer to come around and look at it in the next few days, even though her heart was pounding a mile a minute at the thought of being alone with him.

She breathed a sigh of relief when Anna fussed about going to bed. "I'm not tired," Anna argued. "And if we don't have school tomorrow, I can sleep in."

"Anna, you'll probably have school tomorrow," Jake said patiently. "Even if you don't, I have to go to work and you'll either have to go with me or to day care. Either way, you'll have to get up early."

She grabbed Christine's arm. "Can I stay with you if we have another snow day?" she begged, her mouth pursed in a pleading gesture.

Christine rubbed the back of her hand down Anna's eager little face. "I have to work, too, honey."

"Will you at least read me a bedtime story?"

"I can do that." She glanced at Jake.

"Go on," he said. "I'll do the dishes while you're gone."

When she came back into the room, no trace of their supper remained. Jake was wiping off the now-empty table. "She asleep?" he asked.

Christine leaned against the refrigerator. He moved with a minimum of effort, reaching across the table with slow, easy strokes. She tried not to think of those same hands touching her, caressing her . . .

She shook her head, blotting out the images, and returned to his question. "She should be asleep soon. She was yawning and rubbing her eyes by the time I finished the story. I think she's still a little excited, though, from her day."

"I figured that much exercise would wear her out." He rinsed the rag in the sink and hung it over the faucet.

"She should sleep fine," Christine said. "Once she gets to sleep."

Jake closed his eyes and rotated his shoulders and head around. "I think I'm getting too old to sled. My body aches all over."

Her massage skills had soothed many a restless patient and her first inclination was to rub the pain away. But she didn't think rubbing Jake's shoulders and back would soothe either one of them.

She kept her hands firmly clenched at her sides. "Maybe you should take a long shower or bath," she suggested. "I'd be happy to take a rain check on the movie."

"Are you breaking our date?" he asked in a mock growl.

A tiny snort escaped her. "A date? Is that what this is?" She couldn't help the cool tone that slipped into her voice.

"I thought so." He gave her a puzzled look. "What's the matter?"

She rubbed a hand over her eyes, pretending a sleepiness she didn't feel. The idea that she could be in love with him pressed against her and she didn't trust herself alone with him until she had figured out what she was going to do about it. "I guess I'm just tired. It's been a long day for me, too. A couple of our nurses couldn't get in today because of the weather and I had to work overtime."

"Are you sure you want to go?"

She nodded. She needed to get home and sort out her feelings. "Yes. Thank you for dinner. It was nice not having to cook."

"No problem." He hesitated for a moment. "I'll get your coat."

He disappeared through the door and she took several deep breaths, feeling more in control by the time he returned with her coat. He held it out while she slipped into it, and then he picked up her boots. When she reached for them, he pushed her into a kitchen chair and lifted her right foot, sliding the boot on easily before buckling it.

She had never felt delicate around a man before but Jake made her feel almost fragile as he knelt in front of her, his hands carefully buckling her boots. *Is this what Cinderella felt like*, she mused, *when the slipper was slipped on?* She wasn't prone to fanciful thoughts but her tiredness and the proximity of Jake seemed to bring it out in her.

He walked her to her car. "You're sure you won't stay?" he asked as she opened the door.

"No. I didn't realize how tired I was until just now." She knew she was being a coward, but she needed time alone to think.

"Okay." He leaned over and kissed her. "Good night. Drive safely."

"So, am I like the biggest jerk or what?" she asked Rocky as she rinsed his dishes in the sink. He sat at her feet, his tail thumping the floor. "I could have had a wonderful evening—ALONE—with him, but no, I had to run away."

She sighed and rested her hands on the edge of the sink. "Do I really love him? Or am I just attracted to him? I mean, when was the last time I had a real date, a real guy who paid attention to me?"

Her brothers had provided her with escorts to several of the town's functions. Their help hadn't been solicited, but she had felt helpless to turn down the poor souls they had commandeered to date their little sister. Afterwards, she had turned on Seth and Luke, informing them she could find her own dates, but they had only laughed and asked her to give them proof.

"Now I find my own date and I can't stick around long enough to see what will happen." She turned off the faucet and picked up the cup of tea she had brewed earlier. She wandered into the living room, Rocky's toenails clicking behind her.

Could she love someone she barely knew? She knew of him, his prowess on the football field, his business ability, his concern for his sister. But did she know enough to make an informed decision?

She snorted at her own thoughts. An informed decision about love. From her friends' experiences, she didn't think logic had anything to do with love. Mandy had been absolutely positive she could never settle down in Durant. If anyone had said that she would be not only living in the town but teaching kindergarten a year ago, her closest and dearest friends would have laughed out loud. And now here she was, settled in a house with a six-year-old daughter and going into a classroom every morning. All because she had fallen in love.

"Aargh!" She dropped on the couch, her hands wrapped around her cup. Was love supposed to be this confusing, this difficult? No wonder there were so many songs and poems written about it. Nobody could figure it out.

The storm didn't materialize. Instead, the weather shifted to an unseasonable warm spell and Jake begged off coming over, saying that he wanted to work outside as much as possible. She accepted the reprieve, knowing it wouldn't last for long.

Thanksgiving morning, a tickling sensation on her feet woke her up. She wiggled her toes and the prickling stopped and then started up again. "What in the world?" She sat up and stared into Rocky's eager face.

"How did you get in here?" She tossed the covers off and stepped on the bare floor, shivering at the cold air. Pausing only long enough to pull on a pair of thick socks, she hurried down the hallway, afraid of what she would find.

The destruction was minor. His gate had been knocked over and the trash can lay on its side. At least she had emptied it before she went to bed. The living room didn't show any signs of damage and the door to the other bedroom was closed.

"Now what am I going to do with you?" she asked, scratching his head. He gave a contented growl and leaned against her leg.

"If you get much bigger," she warned him as she opened the back door, "you can't live in this house. It won't be big enough for the both of us."

Her warning didn't seem to bother him. He bounded across the yard, stopping to bark at a cardinal sitting on the fence and then racing to the back corner where he ducked behind a thick bush. Just as if he needed his privacy, she thought with a grin, closing the door behind him.

She lingered over her coffee and the paper, enjoying her morning off. Two pumpkin pies and a pecan one sat on the counter, ready to go to her parents' house that afternoon. She had spent the evening before baking, unable to settle down with her book or the television. Work had kept her mind occupied during the day but as soon as she left the hospital, she found herself thinking about Jake. She hadn't seen him since their dinner together, but her sleep had been disrupted by thoughts of him. Even reading the paper brought his face to mind when she saw that he had applied for another building permit.

Rocky scratched at the door and she let him in. "I'm going to have to lock you in the bathroom when I leave," she informed him. "I don't think you'll like it as much."

He whimpered and scratched at the door when she closed him in and she winced. When the weather warmed up, she could leave him outside. If she could be sure he would stay in the yard. The fence had held him so far, but he was growing bigger every day.

Picking him out at the shelter, she had never dreamed he would get so big. Luke had warned her that he would grow into his feet and paws, but she had been adamant that she wanted the scruffy little puppy with the big brown eyes. Even if she had known for certain that he would grow as big as he seemed to be, she wasn't sure she would have been able to leave him behind. Something about his eyes had tugged at her heart and she had known he was the one for her.

Just like she knew Jake was the one for her. The thought crystallized and she felt a peace enter her mind. Some things didn't need to be analyzed. They just were.

Whistling, she carried her pies up the back steps and banged on the kitchen door with her elbow. "Hello?"

The door opened. Her brother Seth grinned and reached for the pies. She tugged them out of his way. "Not until dessert." She pushed past him and added them to the collection on the far counter.

"Just a taste?" he begged.

She shook her head. "You know what my pies taste like."

"I know what they tasted like last year. This year, they could be different." He lowered his head toward hers. "What if they aren't any good? I could save you some embarrassment."

"Good try but no." She batted at his hands and positioned herself between him and the pies. "Mom!"

Catherine hurried into the kitchen. "Good grief, you'd think you were kids again." She frowned at Seth. "Are you trying to get to the pies?"

Christine gave him a smirk. "He was, Mom."

"Well, get out of here, both of you. The game's on."

"Don't you want Christine to help?" Seth asked from the doorway. "Fixing dinner is woman's work, isn't it?"

She stuck her tongue out at him. "You know how to baste a turkey," she said. Her parents had never divided the chores in the household by gender. They had all taken turns with the laundry, cooking, mowing the lawn, and the myriad of other chores involved in running a house.

Their mother flapped her apron at them. "Go! Before you both drive me crazy. As if you haven't all ready," she muttered.

Christine bent and kissed her mom's cheek. "Sorry. We'll leave you alone."

Her father and Luke were already seated in front of the television set. "No!" Luke jumped from his seat and shook his fist at the screen. "Did you ever see such a call?" he asked the room at large. "What is the ref doing?"

Christine pecked her dad's cheek and perched on the arm of his chair. "So, who's winning?"

"The bad guys," her dad said, his gaze never leaving the game.

"Too bad." She studied the screen, checking positions. "What's going on?"

Luke sat down again and frowned at the screen. "Franklin hasn't completed a single pass."

They watched the game in companionable misery. Catherine joined them for a few minutes, adding her comments to those of the group gathered around the set.

The doorbell rang just as their receiver made it across the goal line. Christine and Seth were doing an impromptu victory dance in front of the couch when Jake and Anna were ushered in by Catherine.

Jake's eyebrow lifted. Christine slipped her hand out of Seth's grasp and backed away from him. "Hi," she said.

"Hi. I take it things are going well."

"We just scored," Luke said, waving a hand at Jake. "Finally. You wouldn't believe the boneheaded plays they've been calling."

Jake sat down on the couch next to Luke. Anna ran up and wrapped her arms around Christine's waist. "Hi."

Christine hugged her. "Hello. I'm glad you came over."

"Me, too." She looked at the television. "Do you like football?" she asked in a loud whisper.

"Christine loves football," her father said. "She doesn't miss a game."

"Really?" Jake leaned back and smiled at her. "I didn't know that."

She didn't know if he was amused or pleased. "It doesn't come up much in conversation."

"It could." He scooted over and patted the empty space next to him. "Sit down."

Her earlier feelings of serenity deserted her when faced with his smile. "I probably should help Mom."

"Mom doesn't want us in the kitchen, remember?" Seth said, a devilish grin on his face.

She didn't dare frown at him, knowing Jake could see her. "That was earlier," she said, mustering all of her dignity. She smiled at Anna. "Would you like to go into the kitchen with me?"

Anna's face lit up. "Yes." She clutched Christine's hand as they crossed the room.

Catherine looked up from her position at the sink, a potato in her hand. "What are you doing in here?" she said, not unkindly.

"Anna thought you could use some help." She didn't mind hiding behind the little girl, not when it afforded her some breathing space.

"Then come here." Catherine reached for another potato and showed Anna how to wash it with the vegetable brush.

They soon had an assembly line going. Anna washed the potatoes, Catherine peeled them, and Christine diced them before dropping them into the pot. They talked and laughed as they worked, Anna chatting about school and Christine sharing stories about Rocky.

"He broke his gate?" Anna asked, wide-eyed when she heard about Christine being woken up by a wet tongue.

Christine nodded. "I had to leave him in the bathroom."

"I hope you moved the toilet paper." Catherine dried her hands and carried the filled pot to the stove.

"The toilet paper?"

Her mother turned on the burner and looked around the room for her next task. "He'll pull it all over the room if you didn't."

Christine groaned. She had moved the trash can and secured the seat lid so he couldn't accidentally fall in. But she hadn't thought about the roll of paper.

"It's okay," Anna said, patting her hand. "At least he won't get bored while he's in there."

The three were still laughing when Paul poked his head around the door. "What's going on in here?"

"We're just finishing dinner," his wife said. "What's happening in the game?"

"Unless we totally blow it," Luke said, coming in behind his father and snitching a carrot from the relish tray, "we should win."

"No game's certain until the last minute," his father said. "Isn't that right, Jake?"

Jake stood behind Paul, his arms crossed over his chest. Christine felt a delicious shiver run through her. She had been around tall men all her life, but Jake seemed to tower over her brothers and father. Little currents of longing arced between them, and she couldn't believe he didn't feel them, too.

He nodded at her father's question. "Amazing how much can happen at the end of a game," he said. He picked up a piece of celery and went back into the living room with the others.

Christine didn't move, watching his broad shoulders as he leaned over the couch, his elbows resting on the back

He chuckled at something Luke said and then his attention was again riveted by the game.

Her mother's voice broke her reverie. "Would you get the milk please, Christine? I think the potatoes are ready."

An excited, noisy group sat down at the dining room table. Their team had held off their opponents and won by a mere three points. "Quite a game," Paul said, taking his place at the head of the table. "Dinner will go down smoother after that win."

"Dad, do you mean you wouldn't enjoy Thanksgiving if our team lost?" Christine reached over his shoulder and poured water into his glass.

He swatted her and she juggled the pitcher to keep from dropping it. "Don't be smarty with your old father."

She laughed and kissed the top of his head. "Well, is that your answer?"

He sobered and looked around the table. Two kinds of salad flanked the bowl of mashed potatoes. A dish of stuffing sat next to a platter of fresh rolls and an empty space in front of him waited for the turkey. "No," he said, "I would enjoy dinner even if we lost." A big grin split the ruddy face that explained why Christine had freckles. "Just not as much!"

Catherine carried in the turkey and carefully placed the platter in front of Paul. She sat down next to him and smiled at Jake and Anna. "Part of our Thanksgiving tradition is to go around the table and say thank you for something before grace. As guests, you may choose to pass or to add to the list."

"I want to," Anna said, glancing at her brother.

Jake patted her shoulder. "So do I."

Luke started, giving thanks for his family, health, and the dedication of his team. Seth mentioned his job and friends in addition to family support. Catherine gave the same list as always: her family, her health, her community. Paul squeezed her hand and echoed the sentiments, adding "and retirement," which brought smiles to the faces of his children.

"It's your turn, Christine," Anna said, bouncing on her chair.

Christine smiled at her. "Family, of course," she said, smiling at them. "And my job, which is going very well." She hesitated, wanting to say what was in her heart. "And new friends," she finally stated, tilting her head so she could see Anna's face.

Anna grinned, showing the gap where her tooth had been only days earlier. "My turn." She knelt on her chair. "I'm thankful for my health, my family, and my stitches."

She beamed at the table. "Anna," Jake said quietly.

She twisted around until she could face him. "What?"

"You're supposed to be serious."

Her eyes widened. "I am." She spun around and her water glass wobbled precariously. Christine righted it with one hand. "I'm thankful for my stitches," Anna explained in a somber voice, "because I met Christine there."

Christine gave her a tight hug. "Then I'm thankful for your stitches, too."

Anna wiggled out of her embrace. "Now you, Jake."

Jake rested his hand over the back of Anna's chair. "I can repeat everything that the rest of you have said. My health, my job. Most of all, though, I have to say, my family. Anna, thank you. You've given me a whole new way of looking at life."

A lump caught in Christine's throat and she turned away, catching the interested gaze of her father. She lowered her lashes and nervously picked at the border of the tablecloth, grateful when her mother asked them to bow their heads for grace.

Dinner progressed with laughter and praises for the meal. Anna kept Christine too busy to worry about Jake, her piping voice asking question after question. She wanted to know every ingredient in the salad her mother had made, finding each item as Christine named it. She let the men at the table know that she helped make the mashed potatoes and that she cooked dinner with Christine one night.

"Jake came over and ate it and he said it was delicious. Didn't you?" She shifted in her chair and looked at her brother for confirmation.

He nodded. "It was good."

Seth pushed away from the table and folded his hands over his stomach. "I can't eat another bite," he announced.

"What about dessert?" Anna asked.

He considered her question and then shook his head. "I'd pop like a balloon."

She giggled. "Then can I have your piece?"

"No." He looked at his mom. "You'll save me one, won't you?"

His mother began gathering the dishes and Paul stood up to help her. "I don't know. You were awfully rude when Christine brought them in earlier."

"I'll be good, I promise. Christine, you'll share your pies with me, won't you?"

"I don't know." She glanced at Anna. "What do you think?"

Anna stretched up until she could reach Christine's ear. One little hand rested on her shoulder. "I think we should share," she whispered. "Otherwise, he might feel bad."

Christine patted her hand. "We're only teasing him," she whispered back.

Anna looked at Seth. "He knows that?"

Christine nodded. Anna settled back on her chair. "Good."

Her parents shooed the rest of them out of the kitchen. "We'll do the dishes and then fix some dessert," her father said. "You relax, enjoy the game, take a walk." He winked at his children. "I want some time alone with your mother."

Seth invited Anna to play a game of checkers with him. Luke flipped the remote, settling on another football game. Jake and Christine stood next to each other a few feet from the table.

"Do you want to take a walk?" Jake asked. "I need to work off a few of these pounds before I have any pie."

She didn't think he had a spare ounce of flesh on him. The thought of a walk, of being alone with him, confused her, but she didn't want to be a coward again.

"I'll get my coat."

They walked down the block in silence, their hands jammed in their coat pockets. The sun had slipped behind the houses, shadowing the street. A light wind blew around them and the few leaves left from fall danced in the street.

"Luke was right. Your mother is a great cook," Jake said as they turned the corner.

"She enjoys it. My dad's pretty good, too."

"I don't remember my dad ever being in the kitchen." He kicked a rock in front of him and when it landed by Christine, she booted it back to him.

"Actually, I don't remember my parents being together very much at all," he said. He absently sent the rock toward the street and it landed with a thud. "They sure didn't act like your folks."

"My folks are pretty special."

They were on the back side of her street and she could see house lights going on Cars lined the streets, testament to the number of people who were visiting. She imagined the families who had gathered together for the holidays.

She rested a hand on Jake's arm. "I'm sure this is hard for you without your parents. Anna's lucky to have you around."

He shrugged. "We never did have the type of family you do. I can't imagine a Thanksgiving like the one we just celebrated at my parents' house."

"Everybody does things differently."

"No." He shook his head and covered her gloved hand with his own. "We didn't do things, period. I'm not sure why my parents even stayed together, unless it was because of the scandal they would have caused here in town if they'd gotten divorced."

She frowned, amazed at the amount of feeling in his voice. They crossed another street. "You know," he continued, "I could hardly wait to get away from here when I graduated. All I could think about was leaving. And then, after Mom moved away and I decided to start my own business, this seemed to be the perfect place. Funny, isn't it?"

"Your roots are here," she ventured.

"Yeah." He kept his hand on hers and led them down another block. "Now that Anna's with me, I'm glad I made that choice."

So am I, she thought. A rush of tenderness welled up in her. Had anyone known the pain he was suffering when he was leading his team to victory? Had anyone seen beyond the football star to the tormented young boy underneath?

She twisted her hand around until her fingers were laced with his. Their hands dropped between them, still linked together. "We should get back," she said softly. "Otherwise, Seth will eat all the pie."

Seth had made inroads on the pies, but Anna had secured several pieces for them. "You said we had to share," she told Christine with a glare toward Seth. "You didn't say he got them all."

Christine laughed. "You better watch out," she told her brother. "You're going to create an enemy here."

"She's just mad because I beat her in checkers." Seth forked up a mouthful of pumpkin pie and grinned over the whipped cream at Anna.

Anna gasped. "He did not beat me!" She scowled and then her lips curved upward. "You're teasing me, aren't you?" she asked Seth.

He reached over and ruffled her hair. "You owe me another game, munchkin. And I'm going to watch your moves like a hawk."

She giggled and plopped down in his lap, sticking her finger in the whipping cream on the last bite of his pie. "I play fair, Seth. You know that."

He dropped his fork and wrapped his arms around her waist. "I don't," he said, tickling her.

She squealed and wriggled around, trying to get away. Christine laughed at them and busied herself cutting a small piece of pumpkin pie and one of pecan.

Jake watched her for a moment. "Is that for me?"

She lifted her head. "You can't use a knife?"

He reached over and took the plate away from her, holding it out of reach when she grabbed for it. "Hey, give that back."

He scooped up a fingerful of whipped cream and wiped it on her nose. "I'm company, remember? You have to treat me nicely."

She rubbed the cream off her nose with the palm of her hand and watched as he calmly picked up a fork and ate a bite of pie. He cut off another bite.

"Open your mouth."

Bemused, she did. He popped the bite in. "Now chew," he instructed, pushing her chin up with one finger until her mouth closed.

Fascinated by this side of him, she did as directed. He alternated feeding her and eating bites himself until they finished the two pieces.

He put the empty plate in the sink. "Anna, are you ready to go?"

Anna stopped wrestling with Seth. "Do we have to?"

Jake glanced at the kitchen clock. "It's getting late, honey. We've been here most of the afternoon."

"You don't have to rush off," Paul said, coming into the room. "We've started a puzzle and we might watch a movie later. Besides, don't you want a turkey sandwich?"

Jake groaned and patted his stomach. "Not in the near future."

Paul chuckled. "You will. I bet you eat a sandwich before you go." He opened the refrigerator and pulled out a can of soda, popping the top as he walked back into the living room. "Convince him to stay, Christine."

Jake looked at her. "Do you want me to stay?" he asked softly.

He stood so close she could see the flecks of brown and gold in his eyes. His breath fanned across her cheek and she caught the scent of his aftershave.

She nodded. She wanted him to stay, to be part of this Thanksgiving and all the others to come.

Chapter Nine

The evening passed in a whirl. A card table had been set up at the edge of the room, across from the sofa, and Paul upended a puzzle depicting a snowy scene straight from a Currier and Ives picture. Jake and Christine sat across from her parents, talking quietly while they worked on the puzzle. Several times his fingers brushed against hers as they searched for pieces, and her breath would catch until he moved his hand. His leg pressed against hers once when he leaned forward to add a piece to the border, and she didn't dare move, unwilling to break the contact.

Luke found an animated movie for Anna and popped it into the VCR. When he sat on the couch, she hopped onto his lap and snuggled against his chest.

"Hey," Seth said, his lower lip pushed out in a pout, "what about me?"

Anna giggled and scooted over until her head was resting against his shoulder. Seth draped his arm over her shoulders and tickled her chin, startling another giggle out of her until

Luke shushed them both. "If we're going to watch the movie, be quiet," he growled.

Seth waggled his eyebrows at his older brother. Anna clapped her hand over her mouth to hold back her giggles before they were engrossed in the action of the movie.

Jake watched them with such a stark look of hunger that Christine's heart ached for him. His words on the walk had stayed with her. She knew he was comparing this evening with evenings he had spent with his own family.

Going with her instincts, she reached over and gave his hand a quick squeeze.

He turned toward her, his eyebrows lifted. "What's that for?" he whispered.

"No special reason." Embarrassed that she had let her emotions show so clearly, she quickly bent her head and picked up a piece of the puzzle, pressing it into an open space.

"It won't go there," Jake said softly, taking it from her hand. "That's the tree trunk and I'm sure you're holding a piece of the sky. At least it looks blue from over here."

She caught the humor in his voice and bit her lip. "You're right, it is blue," she said, determined to act nonchalant. "Must be the lighting."

When Catherine excused herself to make sandwiches for the group, Jake offered to help. He gave Christine's shoulder a gentle squeeze as he stood up and she raised her head, surprised, watching him disappear into the kitchen.

"Here. This goes on your side." Paul handed her a puzzle piece and she studied the scene before snapping it into one of the houses that dotted the landscape.

Her father moved several pieces around, arranging them

by color at the edge of the design. "I like him," he said, giving her a piece that completed another house.

"I do, too," she said quietly. Her father knew her too well to be put off by any pretended confusion at his statement on her part.

"Anything I should know about?"

She shook her head, her eyes still on the puzzle. "No. We're just friends."

"Friends." Her father didn't snort, but she could hear the disbelief. "That young man thinks of you as more than a friend."

She hoped her father was right. Except for the few times when Jake had touched her hand while working the puzzle, he hadn't made any overtly possessive gestures around her family. But he had stayed close to her side, including her in his conversation and asking her opinion about several topics.

He fit in with her family, sharing in the ribbing and teasing that were as natural to her brothers as breathing. She could hear him chatting with her mother and when he carried out a platter piled high with turkey sandwiches, he accepted their gratitude with a grin and then nabbed two sandwiches before her brothers could get to the plate.

She didn't want to make assumptions. They had been thrown together because of his sister and, except for the cross-country meet and their walk earlier in the day, she had never been alone with him. Part of that was her own fault, she acknowledged, but she was wary of reading too much into one evening.

"Here." He handed her a sandwich and sat down on the arm of her chair. "How long does it usually take you to finish a puzzle?" he asked Paul, easily sliding a piece into place with his free hand.

"We'll leave this up until Christmas. Usually everybody that comes over finds a piece or two that fit." Paul grunted when the piece he was holding didn't fit.

"It goes here." Jake pointed to an empty spot on the opposite side of the picture.

The piece snapped in easily. "You've got a good eye," Paul said.

Jake's gaze caught hers for a moment before he turned back to her father. "Thanks," he said quietly.

Time stopped while she watched the back of his head, barely able to breathe. As the sounds of the room faded from her consciousness, she could only hear the steady rise and fall of her own breath.

"Movie's over," Luke said, breaking the spell. He crossed the room and bent down, clicking off the television before pushing the rewind button on the VCR. When he stood up, he stretched and gave a big groan.

"Shh, Anna's asleep," Seth whispered. He twisted around so he could see over the back of the sofa. "Want me to put her in the spare room?"

Jake stood up. "No, I'll take her home."

"It's not a problem," Catherine said. "Why not let her sleep here and have breakfast with us? You can pick her up around lunchtime."

"We'll have more turkey sandwiches," Paul offered.

Jake laughed. "Oh, that's hard to resist. But I don't want to impose."

"You're not imposing." Catherine rested her hand on his arm, her smile gentle as she looked up at him. "When did you last have a night off, Jake, without worrying about her?"

His jaw tightened. "She's not a problem."

"I know, that's not what I meant. But even parents take

time off every now and then.'' She nodded at Seth, who stood up with the sleeping little girl in his arms. ''She'll be fine. I'll listen for her so she's not disoriented in the morning. You go home and just enjoy your evening.''

''If you're sure . . .''

Christine could hear him wavering. ''Mom will love having a child in the house again,'' she added. ''And with Anna around, maybe she'll quit bothering the three of us to get married and have children.''

As soon as the words left her mouth, she wished she could bite off her tongue. Luke grinned at her and then busied himself popping out the tape and putting it back in its case. Seth's reaction showed in the muted jiggling of his shoulders. She closed her eyes and counted to ten before opening her eyes and giving Jake a tight smile.

''She'll be fine,'' she said. She turned away from him and kissed her mother's cheek. ''It was great, Mom, as always. I think I'll head home. It's getting late.''

''Do you work tomorrow?'' Catherine released Jake's arm and wrapped her arm around Christine's shoulders, walking with her to the closet where the coats were hung.

''No, but I do work Saturday. I have a list a mile long for tomorrow.''

She shrugged into her coat and then bent down to kiss her father. He tipped his head, his eyes on the puzzle. ''Don't finish this before I come back,'' she warned, tapping the completed portion of the picture.

He chuckled, still concentrating on the puzzle. ''Your mother will have the lights out ten minutes after everybody leaves. A man retires and he still can't call his evenings his own.''

''If you slept in, I might consider it,'' his wife retorted.

"He still gets up at the crack of dawn," she informed Jake. "As if he had places to go and people to see."

Paul muttered under his breath and Christine gave him a quick hug before letting herself out of the house. The air had cooled down and a crisp wind blew against her cheeks as she hurried down the steps and toward her car. Clouds scuttled across the sky, playing peek-a-boo with the moon.

She was unlocking her car door when she heard footsteps behind her. "So, what should we do?" Jake asked.

She turned around, a gloved hand pressed against her chest. "What?" she asked in a breathless voice. She had expected one of her brothers, and the sight of Jake's tall form, silhouetted against the dark shadow of the house, did alarming things to her senses.

"You didn't think I was just going home alone, did you?"

"Well . . ." The thought had crossed her mind, once Anna was bedded down in the spare room, that they could have some privacy. But he hadn't said a word to indicate that he wanted to be with her.

"Christine." He loosely wrapped his arms around her shoulders, his hands linked behind her neck, and held her in place. "Anna is sleeping over and the night is still young."

"We're in Durant, remember?" She could feel her pulse speeding up, warming her even as the wind whipped her hair around her face. "Everything's closed."

"We don't need anyplace special."

Alone with Jake. She swallowed. "I need to let Rocky out. Who knows what he's done to the bathroom." She knew she was babbling, but she couldn't stop. "Would you like to come over for some coffee? And I kept a pie at home.'' *Just in case,* she had told herself, refusing to admit why she wanted one available.

''Sounds great. I'll follow you.''

Only a few cars were on the road. His lights reflected off her mirror, a steady reminder that he was behind her. It required all of her powers of concentration to pay attention to her driving.

Their footsteps crunched on the frozen ground as they walked toward her front door. Rocky let out a chorus of greetings, howling and yipping until she opened the bathroom door. His feet slid across the floor as he raced past her and all but fell at Jake's feet.

''Well, there's loyalty for you.'' She opened the cupboard above the sink and took down the coffee and coffee pot.

''I'm just a new smell.'' Jake bent down and scratched Rocky's ear. The puppy flopped on the floor and rolled on his back. Jake obliged and rubbed his tummy.

''You're a pushover.'' She measured coffee into the machine and plugged it in. ''Let him out or we'll have a mess to clean up.''

Jake chuckled and opened the back door, barely moving out of the way before the furry streak raced by him. ''Man, the temperature's dropped,'' he said, shutting the door.

Christine murmured a noncommittal ''hmm.'' The room felt as warm as an oven. She busied herself cutting the pie and slid a piece onto a plate.

''Where's yours?'' he asked when she handed him the plate.

She didn't think she could swallow a thing with him in her kitchen. Her hands were damp with nervousness and she wiped them on her pants, keeping her gaze away from his mouth. If she moved forward just an inch, she would be able to kiss him.

"I'm full from dinner," she said quickly, opening another cupboard and grabbing two mugs. She filled them with coffee and carried them over to the table, wondering if she would even be able to make a pretense of drinking her coffee.

"I had a great time," he said, using his fork to scrape up the last crumbs of the pie. "I'm glad Luke invited us."

"So am I," she said, tracing a pattern on the tabletop with her finger.

"Are you?" he asked softly.

She lifted her head and saw the intent in his eyes. A delicate shiver went through her. He moved forward slowly and she waited, her hands in her lap. When his lips touched hers, she sighed and leaned toward him, sliding her hands up his arms and locking them behind his neck. His hands framed her face and she closed her eyes, giving herself up to his kiss.

The kiss lasted no more than a heartbeat, and yet it seared itself all the way down to her toes. When he lifted his head, she had no doubts left.

She loved Jake Reynolds.

Her lashes half-lowered, she shifted away from him. Her heart hammered in her ears and her pulse skittered alarmingly. Only the thought that he might feel the same way gave her the courage to raise her head.

He was sitting across from her, his elbows on the table and his hands loosely clasped together. If she reached over, she could cover those hands with her own, absorb his warmth, his strength, press her lips against his.

Before she could move, he cleared his throat and she carefully met his gaze. *This is the moment,* she thought, *that first awkward one when you try to express your feelings.*

"You know, Christine, I've been thinking."

Her cheeks flushed at the warm look in his eyes. "Really?" Her voice cracked and she swallowed, running her tongue around dry lips.

"Yeah." He nodded and tipped his head to one side, studying her with dark eyes.

Her heart pounded in her chest. *This is it.* She straightened her shoulders, determined to let him have his say before she said anything.

He ran a hand through his hair and she bit back a grin at his nervousness. He looked sweet and adorable and disoriented. Her heart overflowed with tenderness at this vulnerable side of him.

She understood how he felt. The first time she had considered the possibility of loving him, she had felt like running away, hiding somewhere until she could sort out the dozens of sensations coursing through her. Not until their kiss tonight had she felt a semblance of peace with the idea.

Later, she thought, *we'll laugh about this.*

Momentarily lost in her reverie of their future together, his next words jolted her back to reality. "Anna needs a woman in her life," he was saying, "someone who's going to be around to answer the questions I don't understand. I mean, babysitters are all right, but they can just up and leave without any notice. She's already had enough loss in her life. She needs some stability."

Christine nodded, wondering why he was telling her this now. She knew Anna was part of his life and she would willingly accept his sister into hers. But after their kiss, she had expected something more personal. Maybe not a declaration of undying love, but something that would let her know he cared for her.

"I'm all she has now," he continued. "After what I went through, it's important that she never feels like she's in the way."

"Of course not, Jake." Christine frowned. Did he think she wouldn't be happy to welcome Anna into their family?

"If we got married, Christine, we could give her a good life. You're good with her and she likes you a lot."

Her mouth dropped open a fraction and she clamped it shut, all visions of a rosy life with the man who loved her disappearing as if a television set had been clicked off. Her back teeth gritted together. Under cover of the table, she clenched her hands in her lap, one thumb rubbing the other as she strove for a semblance of calm.

"You want to marry me because of Anna?"

"I have to consider her, Christine. She's part of my life now. And you'd be a good mother to her."

Christine gave one sharp nod. "Of course."

He smiled and settled back in his chair. "Whoo! That went easier than I expected. I wasn't sure, when I first thought about it, whether I should even bring it up. But after I saw the way Anna fit into your family today and how easily they accepted her . . ."

"You decided, why not get her a family of her own?" Christine supplied when he paused.

He nodded, but his brows lowered, the smile disappearing from his face. "Hey, you're not upset, are you? Don't you agree this would be a good thing for Anna?"

"Anna maybe. But what about me? Do you think I want to get married just to be somebody's mother?"

"No," he began cautiously, "and that's not exactly what I meant. It's not just because of Anna. I mean, you and I get along great together. We can talk about things, we have common interests . . .'' His voice trailed off.

''And you think that's enough to get married?''

''Why not?''

She planted both palms on the table and leaned forward, annoyed when he backed away from her. Confusion flickered in his eyes and she focused on that. She would have time enough after he left to deal with the pain rushing through her.

''Did you have a good time at my folks' house?''

He nodded, his eyes wary. ''Do you know why it's so easy to be at my parents' house?'' she asked.

''Because they like people?'' he guessed.

She nodded. ''That, and the fact that they have a lot of love to share with those people.'' She half-rose in her chair, keeping her gaze fixed firmly on his. ''They love each other, Jake, and they loved each other when they got married. That love just naturally spills over to others—their children, their friends, their guests.''

''Okay,'' he said slowly. He shifted in his chair and she felt a quiver of satisfaction. She wasn't going to be the only one uncomfortable in this room.

She left her chair and paced to the sink, resting her hands on the counter and staring out of the window into the night. Rocky ran across her line of vision, his legs pumping up and down. She brushed a hand over her eyes and smoothed her hair behind her ears, buying time as she tried to control her anger.

''That's what I want,'' she finally said quietly. ''A marriage needs two people who love each other to succeed. It's hard enough to have a lasting relationship these days. If there isn't mutual respect—''

''I respect you,'' Jake interrupted. He grabbed her shoulders and swung her around to face him. "I think the world of you, Christine. There's nobody else I would even consider marrying."

"Well, thank you, I guess." She closed her eyes, reliving those moments when he had held her in his arms and kissed her. Had he been playing a part, trying to convince her, or maybe himself, that they would suit as a couple?

She wrenched herself away from him and moved several feet away. "Respect is important, but it's not enough. What if you meet somebody later and you fall in love? Then what happens to Anna?"

Or me? she added silently. *What happens if we do get married and you find out I love you? Would you pity me or would you try to find some feelings for me after all?*

"It won't happen, Christine," he said. "If I'm married to you, I wouldn't look at another woman. I would respect you and the vows we would take. Our marriage would be serious to me, Christine."

She believed him, but she couldn't do it. Knowing that he didn't love her would kill her a little every day. Even having him around, being able to share every day with him, eating together, watching Anna grow up, wouldn't be enough. She wanted what her parents had, what she had always assumed would be hers sometime in the future.

"It wouldn't be enough, Jake." She heard the tremor in her voice and she swallowed, hoping the tears would stay at bay for another few minutes until she could get rid of him. "I'm sorry, but I can't marry you. Maybe I'm crazy or unrealistic, but I need romance in my life, love, mutual caring that goes beyond what you might feel for a live-in babysitter."

"Christine, that's not what you'd be. I've done this all wrong."

She gave him a sad little smile. "No, you've done it right. It's better to get this out in the open before we go any further. At least I know what you expected out of our relationship. Now that you know what I expect, you can see that it won't work."

He opened his mouth and she lifted her hands toward him, shaking her head. "I deserve to be loved by the man who becomes my husband. I've waited this long, Jake. I can keep waiting."

She edged around the table toward the doorway, careful not to let herself bump against him. "I hope it won't upset Anna too much, but I'm not sure I should watch her anymore. I wouldn't want her to get attached to me and then have you marry someone else."

"I'm not going to marry someone else," he said stubbornly. "I never even thought about getting married until this afternoon."

"I guess I should be flattered," she snapped, her nerves frayed. "Or was it because of my mom?"

"No!" His own temper seemed barely controlled. She felt a minute flicker of satisfaction at the chink in his cool facade. "I mean, the atmosphere did make me think about marriage, but it was you who decided me."

"Why, thank you, I suppose." She waved her arm toward the living room and pointed toward the front door. "Now, if you don't mind, I have a busy day tomorrow and I'd like to get some sleep. Much as I'd like to continue this scintillating conversation, I think we've said everything that needs to be said."

Her sarcasm wasn't wasted on him. He grabbed his coat

from the chair where he had tossed it and flung it over his shoulders. She shrank against the wall as he stomped through the archway, his shoulders perilously close to touching her.

"I didn't mean to offend you," he muttered as he reached the front door. "I thought that we would get along great. And you can't deny the attraction between us."

His voice had lowered to a husky whisper and her traitorous body responded. Her lips tingled, her breath hitched in her chest, and she barely stopped herself from leaning toward him for a kiss.

She clenched her hands at her sides. At least she would keep her dignity intact. She shrugged and gave him a smile. "A few kisses, Jake. That doesn't mean much."

His eyes darkened and she swallowed, his blaze of anger leaping across the distance and flicking her skin. Without another word, he slammed out of the house.

She squeezed her eyes shut, holding in the tears. When she heard his car start, she slid the chain into place and clicked off the living room light. Trodding across the dark room, she headed for the light of the kitchen and let Rocky into the house.

The puppy jumped at her legs and she sank to the floor, burying her face in his soft fur. The tears flowed down her cheeks, dripping onto his coat until it was shiny with moisture. She sniffed and lifted her head, wiping the back of her hand under her nose.

"Now what, Rocky? It's not like I'll never see him again. The town isn't that big."

Greg's words about going somewhere else came back to her. Nurses were needed all over the country. If she sent out applications that weekend, she could probably have a new job by Christmas. She could spend the holiday with her family, pack up her few belongings, and start a new life with the new year.

"Is that what you really want?" she asked herself sternly. "Do you want to run away just because he offered you marriage without love? At least you found out before you married him. What if he had pretended to care about you, and then you found out after the ceremony was over?"

Rocky cocked his head, whimpering through her tirade. She ran her hands over his ears and scratched him on the neck. "Come on, boy, let's go to bed." She stood up and he followed her down the hallway, sitting in the bathroom doorway while she washed her face and brushed her teeth, and then padding along with her into her bedroom.

He sat by the closed door while she changed into pajamas, only advancing into the room when she crawled into bed. Tucking the covers around her, she found herself looking into his bright eyes. At his quizzical look, she gave a tiny grin.

"No, I haven't lost my mind. I just need some company. But you can't eat a single pair of shoes, understand?"

Comforted by his presence, she clicked off the light. Folding her hands under her head, she lay back on the pillow, listening as he walked over to a corner of the room and circled three times before dropping to the floor. He gulped in air and then his breathing slowed as he fell asleep.

She stared at the ceiling, watching the play of shadows. The wind whistled through the trees, rattling branches against her windows. When a car backfired in the distance, she jumped. Her elbow hit the headboard and tears sprang to her eyes.

Smothering a sob, she rolled on her side and clutched the pillow to her chest. "Just tonight," she whispered, tears streaming down her cheeks. Just tonight she would cry for what might have been.

Chapter Ten

Christine carried in another bowl of chips and lowered herself to the floor. "Okay, tell us," Mandy said, sprawled on the carpet next to the couch. She pushed her glasses up and grinned at Christine. "What's this about you and Jake Reynolds?"

Christine frowned at Mandy, who quickly raised her hands. "I didn't say a word. Honestly, Christine. Come on, this is Durant. Did you really think no one would find out?"

"I heard you were at the pizza parlor with him." The other woman in the group reached into the bowl and pulled out a handful of chips. "But I didn't want to be rude and gossipy like Abby, so I didn't ask."

"Thanks a lot, Tessa!" Abby laughed and picked up a pillow from the couch, tossing it across the circle. Tessa caught it easily and settled it behind her back.

Christine watched her friends laugh and tease, wondering if she would ever feel as carefree again. Even with the required bunny slippers on her feet, she felt about a hundred years older than her friends. Their get-togethers had started during high school, a monthly evening of laughter and snacks, sometimes a movie, and always lot of talking. Mandy and Abby were now married but that didn't stop them from joining their friends. Except for their years at college and Mandy's stint in Kansas City, they had maintained the ritual.

"Are you okay?" Mandy whispered under the cover of the teasing of the other two.

Christine nodded. "I'm fine." She picked up her soda glass and quickly drank it down.

The bubbles lodged in her nose and then her throat. Before she could stop herself, a burp erupted from her lips. Abby and Tessa froze, their eyes wide as they stared at her.

"Was that you?" Tessa asked, her dark eyes wide.

"Christine! How unladylike!" Abby frowned in a disapproving way, but laughter danced in her eyes.

The corners of Christine's mouth curved upward and then she was rolling on the floor, laughing and giggling as the others tickled and teased her. She finally spun away from them and sat up, fending them off with a raised hand.

"I've never heard you burp before." Tessa slouched against the couch, her long legs stretched in front of her, bunny slippers on her feet.

"I'm not perfect," Christine said, her nose in the air.

They all laughed. "Nobody ever said you were perfect," Mandy agreed when the laughter subsided. "We just thought you had better manners."

"I do. I just drank my soda too fast." She tapped the empty glass and then reached for the bottle sitting on the table at the side of the couch.

Abby snatched the bottle out of her hand before she could pour it. "I think you've had enough, young lady!"

"It's pop." She made a grab for it, but Abby whirled it away and handed it to Tessa.

She wagged a finger at Christine. "You have to pay a price."

Christine put her glass on the floor and crossed her arms over her chest. This was as familiar as the freckles on her nose. Abby always extracted a price, usually asking them to perform a silly routine or sing a song before they could have the item. She didn't know any other CPA with such a wild sense of humor, but the dichotomy of Abby's two sides was what made her such a fun person to have around.

"Okay, what?" She grinned at the others and waited.

"Hmmm." Abby tipped her head up and rubbed a hand under her chin, her eyes narrowed shut. She glanced at the bottle and then Christine's empty glass. "Thirsty, right?"

Christine nodded. She could go into the kitchen and get one of the other bottles of soda she had bought for the evening, but that wouldn't be as much fun.

"Okay, I've got it." Abby dropped her hands to her lap. "Tell us about your Thanksgiving."

Christine gave her friend a startled look. "What?"

"Thanksgiving. What did you do on Thanksgiving?"

She gave their other friends a confused look. This wasn't like Abby's usual requests. "I went to my folks' house, ate turkey, and watched the football games." She reached her hand toward the bottle Tessa held in her lap.

"Nope." Abby took the bottle away from Tessa and slid it behind her back. "Not enough. Tell us about Jake and Thanksgiving."

Christine's mouth went dry. Jake. She had tried to banish Jake and Thanksgiving from her mind, almost convincing herself that he hadn't been there, that he hadn't made that outrageous proposal, that she hadn't shouted at him.

"He came to my folks' house, ate turkey, and watched the football games," she said, hoping her voice sounded light and carefree.

Abby shook her head, looking at the other two for support. She swung her gaze back to Christine. "Something happened. As your best friends, we need to know if we're going to help you."

Christine only wished they could. She hated this sinking feeling in the pit of her stomach, the pain that woke her up at night, causing her to sit up straight and stare at shadows.

But her feelings were still too raw to discuss, even with her best friends.

She shrugged her shoulders and leaned back on her elbows. "Nothing happened, Abby. So, do I get a drink or not?"

Abby hesitated. Christine met her gaze steadily, even while her heart was beating a rapid tattoo under her sweatshirt. She almost breathed a sigh of relief when Abby handed over the bottle. She concentrated on pouring the liquid into her glass, hoping her hand wouldn't shake. If Abby had persisted, she probably would have broken down. These were her best friends and it might help to talk about it.

She saw the concern in their eyes as she lifted the glass to her lips. She took a tiny sip. It tasted as dry as dust. It wasn't healthy to keep her feelings locked up. She knew she could trust the three women in the room with her life.

She put the glass down and licked her lips, clenching her hands in her lap. "Okay, something did happen. He asked me to marry him."

The squeals were just what she had expected. "Nothing happened?" Abby exploded, her hands gripping Christine's arms. "Nothing happened?"

"I turned him down," she said before their excitement overflowed.

Three pairs of eyes stared at her over three gaping mouths. Mandy recovered first. "You turned him down?" she asked slowly.

Christine nodded. This was the part that hurt the most. "He didn't want to marry me because he loves me. He's looking for someone to care for Anna."

"He said that?" Tessa flicked her dark braid over her shoulder. "He said he wanted a mother for Anna?"

Christine nodded, reliving again that horribly jarring moment when she had been brought back to earth. "He said that since I'm so good with Anna, why not get married and take care of her together?"

"But why get married?" Abby toyed with the rim of her glass, running her finger over the top as she watched Christine, all humor gone from her face.

"So she doesn't feel like she's always around babysitters." She wrapped her arms around her bent knees. "He really cares about his sister," she said half to herself, "and he wants her to know some security."

"And that's why he wants a wife?" Tessa asked. "A wife could divorce him, leave them both. Wouldn't that be as traumatic as losing a babysitter?"

"A wife wouldn't leave as easily as a babysitter could," Abby said, speaking from experience. Her own travails with day care services in the area were known to all of them. Since the birth of her daughter two years ago, she had been working out of her home and only used babysitters when it was necessary for her to leave town or during tax season. Even then, she found it difficult to find somebody reliable and trustworthy.

"You have to admit," she told Christine, "you would be a great babysitter to have around."

"Thanks," she said dryly. The compliment only added to her misery.

Mandy wrapped an arm around her shoulders. "You love him, don't you?"

Christine nodded. A week of sleepless nights still hadn't gotten her used to the idea. "Yeah. Otherwise, I probably would have considered his proposal. For about two minutes," she told them when they gasped. "I'm not totally hopeless."

"So, what did you tell him?" Abby scooped up a handful of chips and munched on them, her eyes watching Christine.

"That I wouldn't marry anyone unless there was romance involved, that I expected more from a relationship, and that I deserved to be loved."

Put that way, her shouted comments sounded almost noble. She gave an inward wince as she remembered how she had probably sounded. Nobility and honor had been the furthest things from her mind. She had only wanted to hurt him as much as he hurt her.

Tessa patted her hand. "You did the right thing, Christine. You can't get married just because he wants a babysitter. If it's right, it will work out."

"She's right," Abby put in. "Don't settle for second-best. I know it hurts now, but you made the right decision."

She nodded, finding some comfort from the love she saw in her friends' faces.

"Come on." She leaned over and picked up the stack of movies they had collected between them. "This isn't a pity party, remember? I can have that on my own."

"Okay," Abby said after a moment. She pointed to the

movie on top. "Now, if you want a real man," she gave an exaggerated sigh and rolled her eyes, "he's the one."

Christine laughed, popping the movie into the VCR. Abby had met her husband when they were in the eighth grade, and neither one had ever had eyes for anyone else. Except for a brief separation during their college years, they had been together. Seeing their love for each other had only intensified Christine's desire to find that same kind of love for herself.

She shifted her feet and tried to focus on the movie. The hero reminded her of Jake. Not so much in the looks department, since the actor was blond and at least twenty years older than Jake. More in the way he moved, the little glances he shared with the heroine, the gentle cadences of his voice.

She sighed. If Greg could find a replacement, she would take her vacation right now. She'd jump on a plane and disappear, forget everything for a week, two weeks. Just lay on the beach, soak up some rays, listen to the ocean waves crashing around her . . .

Caught in her fantasy, she blinked and jumped when the lights came on. "Wow, you really got into that," Abby teased, pushing the rewind button on the VCR. She glanced at her watch. "I should probably go. Tim won't go to bed until I'm home."

"Really?" Tessa waggled her eyebrows

Abby grinned and arched her own eyebrows. "Really."

Tessa wrapped an arm around Christine's shoulder. "Well, you poor dears, you go on home to your husbands. We'll just enjoy our freedom together."

"You know, they say single people are jealous of married people." Mandy added empty glasses to the empty bowl of chips she was holding.

"And married people are jealous of single people," Tessa said. "I read the same article. Both groups envy what they don't have."

"Or know." Abby followed them into the kitchen, empty soda bottles in her arms. She dropped them into the trash container. "I love Tim dearly, but I have to admit that sometimes it would be nice to come home and just curl up with a good book, not worrying about what he's going to do."

"That would last about five minutes," Mandy said for all of them. "Abby, dear, you haven't breathed without Tim around for most of your life."

"Well." She stuck her nose in the air, but the effect failed when her glasses slipped down. She poked them up with a finger. "So I like being married. And I found him early in life. Is that a crime?"

Christine hugged her. "Not at all. And you just keep on being happy. That's what we want for all of us, right?"

After they left, she wandered around the house, straightening pillows, putting a magazine back on the rack, carrying a forgotten glass into the kitchen. She trailed her finger over the shelf of books, idly studying the titles she had collected over the years. What would it be like to see someone else's choices next to hers? Would they blend together or would they clash?

She didn't know what types of books Jake read. The only books she had seen at his house were those that Anna owned. Of course, she hadn't prowled around his house, inspecting his belongings, poking into his private spaces.

She sank down on the couch. "Okay, stop this!" She used the stern voice her mother employed whenever she wanted her children to shape up. "You can't keep moping around. You didn't ask to love Jake, but there it is. You can either learn to live with it and put it aside, or you're going to be miserable for the rest of your life."

Misery sounded pretty good. She had told her friends she wasn't having a pity party, but she hadn't had one for a long time. She couldn't remember the last time she had wallowed in frustration at the way her life had turned out. Surely she was due some time.

The movie at the bottom of the pile caught her eye. She gathered a box of tissues, popped some popcorn, and released Rocky from his exile in the back room. "But you can't try to cheer me up," she warned him. "I've earned this."

She caught his paws as he jumped up and tried to lick her face. "No. Even if I wasn't feeling low, you can't do that. You mustn't lick people in the face." She nuzzled her chin along the soft fur above his collar. "Now, come on."

He curled up at the end of the couch and tucked his chin between her feet, sneezing when his nose bumped against the floppy ears of her bunny slippers. She pushed the remote button and watched as a young Audrey Hepburn, luminous as always, enjoyed a perfect day with a man totally wrong for her. "You'd think we'd learn, wouldn't you?" Christine murmured, wiping away a tear. The pile of tissues on the floor was growing with each minute. She knew the way the movie ended and it only added to the poignancy.

When Gregory Peck walked away, his back straight, his eyes only slightly clouded by pain, she gave a huge sigh and sat up, snapping off the television. Rocky moaned and shifted, resettling himself without her feet as a pillow. "So, what happened then?" she asked the slumbering puppy. "Did they just go back to life as usual? Did they always carry a picture around in their heads? How do people go on, knowing that something they really wanted isn't available?''

She frowned at the blank television screen. She wasn't a princess in love with a reporter. She was a small-town nurse in love with a contractor. Was that so impossible? If he cared enough about her to have her take care of his sister, why couldn't he care about her for himself?

She cradled Rocky in her arms and settled him for the night, ignoring his sleepy protests. Rinsing out the last of the dishes and turning on the dishwasher, she padded into her bedroom. Crawling under the covers, she studied the shadows on the ceiling before rolling over and closing her eyes. She'd think about it tomorrow.

Her day moved slowly, with one minor crisis after another. In the middle of the afternoon, she took advantage of a lull and went down to Greg's office. He assured her that they had received a few applicants for the nursing positions, but he asked her to hold off on her vacation. ''You said I needed to get away,'' she reminded him.

He ran his hand through his hair. His usually immaculate desk was covered with papers. She couldn't even see the mint jar. ''I know.'' He waved his hand over the piles of papers, almost as if he hoped they would disappear. ''But things are rather strained right now.''

''Fine.'' She turned away and then paused at the door. Biting her lower lip, she turned toward him. ''I'm sorry, I didn't mean to be rude. But I do need some time off.''

''Then take a day. I'm sure we can cover that.''

She shook her head. ''I need more than a day, Greg. I need to get away for a while.''

He nodded and she could see the concern in his eyes. She wondered what Mandy had told him. She knew her friend wouldn't gossip about her, but she didn't think that applied to a husband. "I'll see what I can do, Christine. That's all I can promise."

She accepted his word and left the office. Upstairs, she found Kelly and Beth staring at a large box that had been delivered to their station. "What's the matter?"

"What are these?" Beth held up a plastic smock.

Christine frowned. "Some sort of painting smock, I think."

"I know, but why do we have them?" Beth dug into the box and emerged with a package of paint brushes. "This is full of art supplies. Are we supposed to do our own decorating now?"

Christine studied the label. "Wait a minute." She brushed at a smudge. "This says Floor 2—not Floor 3." She frowned and then smiled. "I know what these are." She gathered up the few items they had stacked on the counter and dropped them back into the box. "I'll be right back."

She carried them down a floor and around the corner to Pediatrics. "I think this belongs to you," she told the nurse on duty.

She popped open the box and extracted a smock and the brushes. "Finally. We wondered when they would arrive." She smiled at Christine. "Have you seen the changes yet?"

Christine shook her head. Her own floor and her hours in the emergency room had taken up most of her time. "Come on."

The nurse led the way down the hall and into a brightly lit room. Windows on two sides brought in the sunshine. A mural showing animals of the world covered the other two walls. Christine could see butterflies and birds peeking around the window sills.

"Who painted this?" she asked.

"The high school art class. They spent a couple of weekends and some after school hours up here." She pointed to the top of a window. "That's my favorite."

A lizard peeked at them, its tiny feet barely visible above the ledge. A curve of tail a few inches away gave the impression that it was hiding behind the wood.

"Clever." Christine surveyed the rest of the room. Bright yellow chairs sat around a red table the size of a child. A blue bookcase held stuffed animals and books. In the far corner, an easel sat on a tiled section of floor. The nurse hung up two of the smocks on hooks next to it and opened a package of paintbrushes.

"The children will love this," she said.

"When Jake Reynolds first mentioned making the room more kid-friendly, there was some grumbling. But once he showed the administrators his plans, they thought it was great. In fact, now you would think it was their idea."

Christine's delight in the room paled. "Jake Reynolds designed this?"

The nurse nodded, intent on organizing the painting supplies. "You remember what this room looked like? We had that one poky old window overlooking the parking lot, and the walls were in horrible shape. They put in these windows, refinished the walls, and added tile to this corner." She rubbed her shoe over the carpeting. "And we finally got some indoor-outdoor carpeting. We couldn't keep that other stuff clean, so it always looked dingy in here."

"Doesn't look dingy now. It looks great."

The nurse straightened a cushion on the full-sized couch, the only indication that others besides children might use the room. She joined Christine in the doorway. "It does, doesn't it? We have the official ribbon-cutting next week and I was hoping everything would be here.''

She stepped into the hallway and Christine followed. ''Mrs. Fletcher is going to cut the ribbon,'' she said. ''She donated most of the money for the renovations.''

''Really?'' She had heard about the changes taking place on the ward, but not all the details. She wished she had paid more attention.

''Will you be at the ceremony?''

Not if Jake would be attending. ''Probably not. But congratulations.''

The afternoon sun hung heavy in the sky when she finally made her way home. Stopping to unlock her door, she found a note attached to the knob. She pushed the door open and detached the heavy card.

''Flowers by Josie,'' she read. Her brow puckered. Who would be sending her flowers? Her family had celebrated her birthday over the holiday weekend and she had received a few birthday cards from aunts and uncles, but she couldn't imagine who would send flowers.

She grinned. Her grandparents. They lived in Florida and refused to return to the Midwest during the winter. No doubt they had sent her flowers to entice her to visit them.

Which was just what she would do if she could ever get the time away. She nudged the door shut with her foot and read the rest of the note. ''We tried to deliver your flowers today, but you were away,'' the bottom of the card read. ''Please see your neighbors next door.''

She dropped her purse on the couch and released Rocky, letting him outside before she walked next door. She had to try both neighbors before she found the right one.

''So, lucky you,'' Mrs. Archer said with a smile. She

carried the gigantic bouquet of roses out of the kitchen and handed it to Christine. "Frank never sent flowers like this to me."

"It's my birthday," Christine explained, wondering what had gotten into her grandparents. They couldn't afford gestures like this on their retirement salary. She would kindly tell them so when she called to thank them.

"Is it a special birthday?" Mrs. Archer's curiosity shone in her eyes.

"Not really. I mean, I was 27 on the 27th." Her grandmother enjoyed puzzles and plays on words, but surely that wasn't why she had sent such a magnificent present.

"Well, enjoy." Mrs. Archer opened the door and waited until Christine was safely down the steps. "And whatever he asks, I'd say yes."

Christine was about to explain that they weren't from a man when the door closed. *Oh, well, she can enjoy the fantasy,* she thought, picking her way over the still slippery patches on the sidewalk.

Opening the door with the heavy vase in her hands took some maneuvering. She carried it into the kitchen and carefully placed it in the center of the table. She draped her coat over a chair and dropped her gloves on the seat.

"I bet they sent twenty-seven roses," she said. She leaned over and counted, frowning when she ran out of roses at twenty-four. "Okay, maybe they only sell roses by the dozen."

Their heady fragrance filled the tiny room. She gently touched one delicate petal and sniffed. Carnations had always been her favorite florist flower, but she thought she could get used to roses.

The furnace kicked on and the sprigs of baby's breath fluttered. She moved the bouquet so it didn't catch the air from the vent and picked up the card tucked between blooms.

The handwriting didn't look familiar, but that didn't surprise her. Her grandparents would have ordered the flowers from their own florist and had the message written by the person preparing the bouquet in town.

She leaned over and inhaled the scent again as she slipped the card out of its envelope. Her eyes half-closed in pleasure, she glanced at the message and then almost dropped the card.

"You want romance?" the card read, the letters dark and bold. "Just watch."

Chapter Eleven

The flowers sat on the edge of the counter and she scowled at them, almost afraid they would come alive and attack her. They had to be from Jake. She couldn't imagine any of her friends playing such a cruel joke on her, knowing how she felt about him.

What did they mean? Was he so concerned about finding someone to help with Anna that he would pretend to woo her? Or did it mean something more?

She couldn't think with the flowers in the same room. Their sweet smell had become cloying and she considered throwing them into the snow. But she paused, her hand hovering over the bouquet. She had never received such a beautiful arrangement and she couldn't make herself get rid of them.

"Besides, someone would see," she muttered, tucking the vase into a far corner of the pantry, "and once word got around . . ." She didn't dare risk the gossips seeing a fresh bouquet of roses in her trash.

For two days, she ignored them, keeping her face turned

away from them whenever she locked Rocky into his corner. But on the third day, when she opened the door and was again greeted by their sharp scent, she knew she couldn't pretend anymore.

"Okay, you win," she grumbled, rescuing the flowers from their corner. She added new water to the vase and centered it on the table. "You're absolutely gorgeous and it was very sweet of him to send you, no matter what the reason."

The petals had opened to their full glory and she inhaled deeply, letting the rich scent seep into her veins. Lightly touching a petal, she marveled at its soft velvety texture. With a rueful sigh and shake of her head at her foolishness, she went into the bedroom and changed out of her uniform.

When she entered the kitchen the next morning, she was greeted by Rocky's excited yips and a burst of rose-tinted air. Her lips curved upward. Amazing how fresh flowers could brighten the day.

She was humming when she walked up to the nurse's station. "Good morning," she said brightly.

"You're in a good mood," Beth said.

"It's a pretty day." She haphazardly sorted through the notes left in her box.

Beth cocked one eyebrow. "A pretty day?" She tapped Christine's forehead. "Hello, it's ten degrees outside."

"So? It can still be pretty. We're alive, aren't we?"

Beth shrugged, giving her a wary look. "Yeah."

She carried her mail into her office. Sitting down at her desk, she picked up the first envelope and slit it open.

Most of the mail required routine handling and she went through it quickly. A letter at the bottom stopped her and she froze, staring at the bold handwriting she had last seen on the card with the roses.

Uneasy, she opened it and slid out the single sheet of paper. She scanned it quickly but there was no signature at the bottom.

Telling herself she was silly to be so worried about a note, she went back to the top of the page.

"Hi!" she read. "I thought you'd like to hear this. A dental hygienist visited Anna's class the other day and talked about tooth care. When Anna came home, she told me, in a very serious voice, that she needed to go to the dentist because she was pretty sure she had a cafeteria in her mouth."

Christine read through it again, her brows drawn together, and then giggled as she reached the last line. "A cafeteria," she sputtered, catching the joke.

"Did you want something from the cafeteria?" Beth asked through the open door.

"No." She glanced at the letter and then called Beth into the room. "It's just that I heard this funny joke." She repeated what Anna had said, leaving out names and how she had discovered the story.

Beth chuckled and went back to her station. Christine smoothed the paper with her finger and traced over the dark letters. Jake hadn't signed his name or used hers but she almost felt as if he were in the room, relaying the story to her.

What did he want from her? Was he trying to show her how much she missed them? He didn't need to do much. No matter how she tried, she couldn't forget their last meeting and the way she had wanted to say yes to his proposal.

Frustrated with herself, she dropped the letter in her bottom drawer and went back to her mail.

The day passed quickly. She spent the evening with her parents, helping her father finish the border of the puzzle.

Twice she started to tell them Anna's story, but each time she paused, afraid they would ask her where the tale came from.

Not once did they ask about Jake. She didn't deliberately keep the news that they weren't seeing each other away from them, but she couldn't bring herself to talk about him. A part of her was afraid that once she did, she would break down and tell them about the proposal. And much as she wanted sympathy, she knew that she wouldn't be able to deal with their concern. She finally rationalized that Luke had invited him for Thanksgiving and that as far as her parents were concerned, her own involvement with them was confined to caring for Anna.

The next morning, she was struggling with a data problem on the computer when the phone rang. She snatched it up quickly.

"Hi, Christine, I was wondering if you could do me a favor."

She recognized the voice of a maternity nurse. "Sure, anything. This new computer program is driving me nuts."

The nurse chuckled. "I understand completely. I think this is a better trade. I'm supposed to introduce the little girl who's cutting the ribbon at the Pediatrics unit today, but the school just called and my son is sick. I don't think it's anything serious, but he needs to go home. So, could you cover for me at the opening?"

"No problem." Christine jotted down the information and hung up, after expressing a wish for a speedy recovery for her son.

The ribbon cutting was in the middle of the afternoon. She walked down to the floor a few minutes before it started. A small crowd had gathered inside the wing and she greeted people as she made her way toward the edge of the group.

"Hi, Christine. I didn't think you were going to make it," a pediatric nurse said.

"I'm filling in," she said with a smile.

"Well, I'm glad you're here. This is a pretty special day for our floor."

"I bet it is. This has been a long time coming."

Jake stood off to the side of the local dignitaries, dressed in a dark suit instead of his customary jeans and jacket. Christine tried to listen to the speeches, staring at the hospital administrator as he thanked Mrs. Fletcher and the others who had contributed to the renovations. After she made her introductions, she kept her eyes focused on the little girl and her parents as they cut the ribbon and tried to clap at the appropriate times. But her attention was constantly drawn toward Jake, even while she told herself that she had to forget about him, that she had to start learning to live in the community without thinking about him every minute.

As soon as the ribbon was cut, she excused herself and quickly fled through the crowd to the elevator. She tapped her foot as she watched the numbers click toward her floor and when the doors slid open, she slipped inside with a grateful sigh.

Just as the doors started to close, a hand pushed them open again. "Hi." Jake slipped in and the doors shut, closing them in the small room together.

"Hi." She stared at her shoes, wishing she'd used the stairs.

"You going back to work?"

She nodded. Her throat didn't seem to work.

"Floor three, right?"

She lifted her head. He was smiling at her, one hand

poised above the panel of buttons. "Yes," she mumbled, feeling her cheeks flush as he stabbed number three and number one. She had forgotten to push her floor.

He stood a few inches away from her, his hands behind his back, his legs spread slightly apart. His hair curled over the collar of his jacket and she could remember the soft, springy feel of it under her fingers. She clenched her hands into fists, tucking them into her pockets.

Should she mention the flowers? Or ask about Anna? He just stood there, whistling softly under his breath, his head tipped toward the ceiling.

When the doors opened on her floor, she practically jumped out of the elevator. "See you later," he said, almost as if they were casual acquaintances.

"Which is what we are," she muttered, combing her fingers through her hair as she marched down the hall to the station. "So why doesn't he leave me alone?"

"So, how did it go?" Beth asked with a curious look on her face.

"What?" She lifted her head and stared at the nurse.

"The ribbon cutting. How was it?"

Christine shook her head, trying to clear her thoughts. "It was fine. They cut the ribbon, thanked everybody. It was nice."

Beth gave her a puzzled look. "Are you okay?"

"I'm fine, I'm fine." Christine backed away and ducked into the nurse's lounge, leaning against the door and taking several deep breaths before she felt calm enough to make it through the rest of her day.

On Monday, she had a meeting to attend at lunchtime and she gave Beth a few last-minute instructions before she left. "I shouldn't be more than an hour," she added.

"Better you than me," Beth said with a shiver. "I hate meetings."

Christine chuckled and walked down the stairs to the main conference room. She agreed with Beth, but as part of management, she had a duty to attend the monthly meetings. Usually the meetings didn't last long. She hoped that would be the case today.

Beth looked up from her typing and grinned when she arrived back at the floor. Angela pointed toward the clock with an exaggerated motion. "I know, I know," Christine said, dropping her notebook into the spot on her desk where it would remain until the next meeting. "We should have finished in an hour. What can I say?"

"You can open the box and relieve our agony," Beth said. She pushed a brightly wrapped package across the counter. "Come on, what is this?"

Christine stared at the package. The same bold handwriting declared that it was hers. "Did you guys do this?" she asked, buying herself some time. Why was he doing this to her? After their exchange in the elevator, she had expected to be left in peace.

"No, we already gave you a birthday present, remember? You're not getting greedy, are you?" Beth grinned and tapped the package again. "Come on, open it. We've been sitting here for over an hour wondering what it is."

Christine wondered how she could diplomatically take the box and open it in privacy. She didn't have a clue about the contents. Jake suddenly seemed like an unknown entity.

She knew she was risking their goodwill, but she couldn't trust herself to open the box in their presence. "I'll open it later," she said, tucking it under her arm. "With that meeting running long, I've gotten behind."

Their faces dropped, but they didn't say a word. After a

moment, Beth turned back to the counter and Angela murmured something about checking on supplies. The package suddenly felt like it weighed a ton and she stifled the urge to toss it in the trash can.

Who are you kidding? she told herself. *You can't wait to see what's inside.*

In the security of the small room she called an office, she tugged off the ribbon and pulled off the top of the box. A white card with the handwriting that was becoming familiar to her lay on top of a box of chocolates. "I didn't know which ones were your favorites," she read, "so I bought all of them. I'll learn soon enough."

She propped an elbow on the desk and rested her chin in her hand. "I'll learn soon enough." She sounded like a project he had undertaken. Was he so determined to get her to marry him that he was willing to learn her habits, her likes, her dislikes?

She opened the chocolates and studied the chart describing the contents. Caramels, dark chocolate, truffles, almonds, nougat, orange creme . . . He had indeed found a box that included every type of chocolate so far invented.

Her hand hovered over a light chocolate covered caramel. It couldn't hurt to just eat one.

"Christine, do you have a minute?"

Her hand dropped away from the box and she cradled the traitorous limb in her lap, giving Beth a bland smile. "Of course, come in."

Beth advanced and then paused, staring at the open box of chocolate. "Is that the package?"

Christine nodded. "Would you like one?" she offered weakly.

"Sure." Beth reached over and plucked a dark chocolate from the middle of a row without referring to the chart.

Sinking her teeth into the morsel, she grinned at Christine. "Sorry. I can see why you were keeping this a secret."

"It's not that I didn't want to share . . ." she began.

"Say, Beth, do you know where that new order of gloves ended up?" Angela leaned in the door and her eyes widened. "Chocolates!"

"Help yourself," Christine said, pushing the box toward the edge of the desk.

"Don't mind if I do." Angela considered her choices for several moments and settled on an oval chocolate that revealed an almond after she took a dainty bite. "This is wonderful. It must have cost a fortune."

The same thought had occurred to Christine. In terms of originality, Jake might not rate many points, but he had gone all out in price. She couldn't imagine where he had found a box of chocolates like this in Durant.

"So, where did these come from?" Beth pressed a finger against her chin and pointed to several of the confections until she carefully picked up a chocolate truffle resting in a lacy cup.

"A friend." Christine picked up a square morsel and popped it into her mouth, hoping they wouldn't expect her to answer with her mouth full.

"A friend?" Beth asked. Both nurses lifted their heads and favored her with a long look. "What kind of friend?"

"Just a friend," she mumbled around the gooey mess in her mouth. The nuts and caramels were making it hard to talk.

"Right." Beth stepped back. "If you don't want to tell us, we understand. We can respect that, can't we, Angela?"

"Sure." Angela wiped her hands on a tissue she pulled from the container on the desk. "I need to finish the supply closet anyway. I have plans for right after work."

"Oh, yeah? What are they?" Beth asked, following her out of the room. "Of course, if you don't want to tell me, that's okay," she said with a glance over her shoulder.

"No, I don't mind at all."

Christine groaned and lowered her head to her crossed arms on the desk. The card lay under them. She had barely been able to hide it before Beth came into the room.

What was she going to do? If he kept sending her presents, word was bound to get out. Even if he was getting the packages from outside town, someone was bound to discover what was going on.

And how could she believably explain that she wasn't interested in Jake when every nerve ending, every fiber, shuddered just looking at his handwriting?

She shoved the card into her drawer, watching it land gently on top of the letter. She crammed the lid back on the box of chocolates. If Angela and Beth liked them so much, they could enjoy them. In fact, all the nurses could enjoy them. She tucked the box under her arm, listening as chocolates slid into the empty spaces, and marched into the nurses' lounge, dropping the box on the table and snapping the lid off so that everyone could see their choices.

She peeked into the lounge just before she went home. Half of the chocolates had disappeared. Satisfied that few would remain by the time she came back in the morning, she left the hospital.

"So, Rocky, now what do I do?" she asked him the next night as she heated up a bowl of soup. "I have two notes, an empty box of chocolates, and a vase of wilting roses. Do I pack them away in a scrapbook as the love that didn't happen? Or is something else going on?"

The wind had shifted and whistled against the side of the house. Wrapped in a thick sweater and with her bunny slippers on her feet, she decided to curl up with a good book and soup, her dog lounging comfortably at her feet, and forget about Jake.

Not that she really expected Rocky to lounge for very long at her feet. He was chasing a chew toy shaped like a mouse around the kitchen, tossing it into the air and then leaping after it. He bopped into her leg and she bumped against the counter.

"Take that out of here," she ordered, opening the back door. "Go on, scoot."

He gave her a pitiful look, his eyes droopy as he looked at the outside and then back to her. "No," she stated firmly, giving him a nudge with her slippered foot. "Go on. You need some fresh air and I need some peace."

Even as she opened the door, she knew she wasn't being fair to the dog. His antics weren't the ones tying her insides into knots. The air blowing into the house was frigid and she shivered in her robe. Rocky slowly padded out of the door, pausing twice to give her sad looks over his shoulder. She didn't relent, shutting the door behind him when he finally reached the edge of the small patio.

Her soup was bubbling and she turned down the burner, opening a cupboard for a bowl. The doorbell rang and she glanced over her shoulder in surprise.

Putting the bowl on the counter, she walked into the living room, knotting the robe around her waist so that her flannel pajamas didn't show. She peered through the peephole and saw a teenager standing on her small porch. A hat advertising the local Chinese restaurant sat on his head and he held two large white bags in his hands.

He reached over and pressed the doorbell again. "I didn't order anything," Christine said through the closed door.

"Are you Christine Hunter?"

"Yes."

"Then this is for you."

"But I didn't order anything," she repeated.

He shrugged skinny shoulders under his letter jacket. "Somebody did. It's all paid for, if that's what you're wondering. Even the tip."

She eased the door partway open. "You don't know who ordered it, do you?" she asked as she took the bags out of his arms. She had an idea but she wanted to hear it from somebody else.

He shrugged again. "Nope. They just told me to deliver it and that you don't owe a thing."

He didn't move. She wondered if he was waiting for another tip. She didn't have any money in her pockets and after a few seconds, he turned around and sauntered down the steps and toward his car.

She closed the door behind him and carried the food into the kitchen, setting the bags next to the roses. The food's aroma overpowered the soup she was cooking and she turned off the burner before peeking into the bags. Unable to resist, she took out several containers and opened them, her mouth watering as she found stir-fried rice, beef with broccoli, sweet-and-sour pork, cashew chicken . . .

She stared at the boxes lining her table. She couldn't possibly eat all of this. He must have ordered food for an army. Or at least two people . . .

Her eyes wide, she stared at the front door and then dashed into her bedroom.

Her sweater settled around her shoulders just as the doorbell rang again. Brushing her hair back from her face with her fingers, she hurried down the hallway and then slowed her pace at the edge of the living room. She pressed her hands against her chest and forced her breathing to slow down. If it was Jake, she was not going to let him know how much she wanted to see him.

His tall figure filled the skewed view through the peephole. She took a deep breath as she opened the door a few inches.

She leaned against the door in what she hoped looked like a casual pose, her hand gripping the doorknob. "Hello, Jake, what brings you here?"

"I was in the neighborhood."

She thought about the times when her brothers dropped by for a meal, making casual conversation, all the while hoping she would invite them to dinner. Two could play games. "Oh, really? It's kind of late for work, isn't it?"

"I had to check on a house a couple blocks away. I thought I'd stop by and see how you were doing."

She nodded. "I'm fine. Tired from work. I was planning to have an early night."

The wind ruffled his hair and he rubbed his hands over his arms. His breath frosted in the wintry air. "Could we take this conversation inside?"

She chewed her lower lip. "I don't know, Jake. I really did want a quiet evening."

"Christine, come on, it's cold out here." He stamped his feet to emphasize his words.

She decided to take pity on him. He had bought her dinner, in a manner of speaking. He had probably waited in the car to make sure it was delivered.

"Okay." She opened the door wider. "But just for a few minutes."

He seemed to fill her small living room and she took a quick step away from him. Once inside, he shrugged out of his coat and draped it over the back of a straight chair in a corner of the living room. "How have you been?" he asked quietly.

"Fine." She wouldn't let him know about her sleepless nights, the confusion he had created with his packages and notes.

"Anna misses you."

A pang lodged itself under her heart. She hadn't meant to hurt the little girl. "I miss her, too," she confessed.

"You know, Christine—"

"No," she interrupted, not wanting to hear him plead Anna's case. Her heart was just starting to heal and she didn't want it ripped apart again by his request to have her see Anna. It would be better if she made a clean break.

"I assume you had this ordered so we could have dinner together," she said briskly, turning her back on him and the dreams she had once cherished, "So, let's eat before it gets cold."

When she entered the kitchen, she wished she had moved the roses to a less prominent place. Sitting in the middle of the table, it was obvious she saw them whenever she walked into the room.

He didn't say anything about the flowers. He sat down in the chair closest to the doorway. She was thankful she didn't have to walk around him to get plates and glasses. She switched on a burner under her teapot and sat down opposite him.

"Thanks for dinner," she said, passing him the rice. "I was warming up a bowl of soup when it arrived."

"Your mother's worried you aren't eating enough."

"My mother?" The bite of rice suddenly tasted like sawdust.

He nodded and helped himself to the cashew chicken.

"We've had dinner with them a few times. Anna and your father are great pals. She's over there right now."

He bent his head, giving his attention to his meal. She frowned at the food on her plate, her appetite deserting her. He had visited her parents. They hadn't said a word when she was over there.

What was Jake doing? She could only see the top of his head, and it gave no clues to the thoughts going on under that thick mane of hair. Was he trying to enlist her parents' support? What had he told them?

She groaned, frustrated by the range of emotions flitting through her. When Rocky whined and scratched at the back door, she jumped to her feet, relieved to have a few minutes to settle her thoughts. If Jake Reynolds was trying to drive her crazy, he was doing a remarkable job at it!

Chapter Twelve

Rocky gave his usual exuberant greeting and then settled in a corner of the kitchen, gnawing on a chew toy he found under the counter. While Jake sampled every item, giving the impression of a man who hadn't eaten in days, Christine tore off tiny pieces of an eggroll and dropped them on her plate.

He finally pushed his plate toward the middle of the table and leaned back in his chair. "So, have you been outside much recently? That warm spell sure helped my schedule."

He wanted to talk about the weather? Didn't he have any idea what his sudden appearance was doing to her? Her plate was covered with shredded pieces of wonton, cabbage, and shrimp, evidence of her agitation. She scooted it away from her. "I'm a little confused," she said slowly. "What are you doing here?"

"What?"

"Why are you over here tonight?"

"I thought we could eat and then I'd look at your door."

He glanced toward the arched opening. "With the weather changing, I should have some time to fix it for you."

She did not want him working in her house. Sitting across from him was hard enough. To watch him moving around her kitchen, making himself at home. . . . She swallowed. "The gate works fine. He hasn't made another escape."

"But he's growing." Jake stood up and crossed the short distance to the entryway. He ran a hand over the textured edge. "It would be a shame to close this off, though. The kitchen would really seem small then."

It seemed pretty small right now, with him standing an armslength away. She could touch his sleeve with her hand without moving from her spot at the table.

She pressed her hands together in her lap. His flowers might be scenting the room and she might have nibbled at food he had provided, but that wasn't enough. What she wanted from him couldn't be bought at a store.

"I may not do anything," she said. "Once the weather changes, he'll spend most of his time outside. Hopefully by next winter, he'll be better trained and I won't have to worry so much about leaving him in the house."

"If you're sure . . ."

She was very sure. She just wanted him out of her house, away from her so she could rid herself of this desire to throw herself against him and beg him to repeat his ridiculous offer.

She swallowed and stacked their dishes together, carrying them to the sink. "I think I'll leave it for now," she stated in what she hoped sounded like a calm voice. "It would change the focus of the room and I'm not sure I'm ready for that."

She turned around and found herself facing his chest. He stood so close she could see the ribbed pattern of his sweater. Perspiration dotted her palms and her cheeks were flushed.

"Christine," he said softly.

She lifted her hands and without conscious thought, rested them on his chest. To push him away, she told herself before she splayed her fingers wider.

"I—this isn't—I don't want . . ." With his warmth beneath her hands, she couldn't form words.

"Shhh."

His kiss was gentle, different than the others they had shared. Her eyes drifted shut and she sank into the comfort he was offering.

"I can't do this," she murmured when he lifted his head.

"What?" He toyed with the hair at her neck and she shivered.

"I can't kiss you. There's no future in it."

"There could be."

She closed her eyes against the pain of losing him a second time and then tried to pull away from him. His arms were locked around her waist, holding her close.

"Jake, please." She hated the way her voice quavered.

"Christine." He lowered his head, but instead of kissing her, he rested his brow against hers. "We need to talk."

"I thought we already did."

"We need to talk again."

He led her into the living room, his hand tight around her wrist. He sat down on the sofa, but when he tried to pull her next to him, she kept her distance, using a bent knee on the seat to keep them apart.

He leaned against the arm of the couch. "I've been thinking."

She regarded him with a speculative gaze. "Really?"

"Christine, this is hard enough without your comments. I'm not used to thinking about my feelings or telling somebody else about them."

"You and the rest of male society," she murmured.

"Christine," he warned, his dark eyes shimmery with an unnamed emotion. "Please."

"All right." She leaned back against the cushion and primly folded her hands in her lap. "What do you want to say?"

"Your reaction to my proposal made me stop and think. I mean, I assumed you would see the advantages just like I did. A business proposition, one that would benefit both of us."

Her facade melted away. "How would it benefit me?" she demanded.

He lifted one hand. "Sorry, but you have to let me finish. I'm just reviewing what happened last time."

As if she needed a review. She settled back in her place, her teeth pressed together. "Anyway," he continued. "Your reaction made me stop and consider what was going on. I mean, why would you be so upset when I offered to marry you unless . . ." He paused and she squirmed under that relentless gaze. "Unless you loved me," he said softly.

She gave a tiny trill of laughter, pleased it didn't sound forced. "Loved you? Well, you have a big ego, Jake Reynolds. Why would I love you?"

He shook his head. "I don't know. I mean, I dupe you into watching my sister, I never do anything with you unless she's around. . . ." He gave another shake of his head. "Except for a few kisses, and that could just be chemistry, I can't imagine why you would love me."

"I'm glad we have that straight."

He reached over and tugged her hands apart, threading their fingers together. "Of course, the same could be said for me. Why would I love you?"

Her heart stuttered. "What?"

He tipped his head up and frowned at the ceiling. "I mean, why would I love somebody who thinks she knows more about raising my sister than I do and always has to have the last word? So what if she's fun to be around, loves my sister, and can kiss like a dream?"

"Jake?"

"Hmm?" He lowered his head and smiled at her.

"What are you saying?"

He tugged her toward him until their faces were only inches away from each other. "I'm saying that these last few weeks have been miserable. I thought I just wanted a business arrangement, no strings attached. But suddenly, when you weren't in my life anymore, I knew that wasn't what I wanted."

"The flowers? The chocolates? The notes?"

"I didn't want you to forget me."

She laughed. "Oh, Jake, I couldn't forget you. I tried, but you're stuck in my head. And my heart," she said quietly.

A long time later, she traced a finger over the veins on the back of his hand. Cradled against his chest, his heart beating steadily under her ear, she felt secure and warm. "I love your hands," she said.

"Really? Is that all you love?"

She raised her hand and lovingly trailed her fingers over his face. "No. Your devotion to your work, your concern for your sister, your stubbornness when you think you're right.'' A contented sigh slipped over her lips. ''I love you,'' she said simply.

''And I love you.''

She snuggled against his side. ''So, now what?''

''Now we get married.''

''Just like that.''

''I thought so.'' He shifted until he could see her face. ''What?''

''Well . . .'' Her lips quirked upward in a grin. ''I just thought . . .'' She hesitated, watching him.

''Wait a minute.'' He dropped his hands from around her waist. ''Do you want another proposal?''

''You have to admit, that first one wasn't exactly romantic. And your note did say you would give me romance.''

He ran his hand through his hair. ''Gee, Christine, isn't there a card I could get for this?''

''It's not that hard.''

''You try it.''

''Okay.'' She cleared her throat and lifted her chin.

''No.'' He pressed a hand against her lips before she could speak. ''I'll ask you. It's the least I can do after the way I treated you last time.''

He rubbed his hand over his chin. ''Christine, I never thought I would say this to any woman. I honestly believed I could be happy without marriage, just doing my job, taking care of Anna. But being around you, I realized that wasn't enough. I wanted something more, something only you could give me.''

Tears pricked the back of her eyes. His voice was so sincere, his expression so tender.

''I didn't realize it right away,'' he said. ''After you first turned me down, I couldn't understand why it bothered me so much. But I missed you, I missed hearing your voice, seeing your face.''

He smoothed a hand over her cheek, his thumb gently caressing her chin. ''Most of all, Christine, I missed the way I felt when I was with you, like I could do anything.''

She captured his wrist between her two hands, holding his hand still. She couldn't think when he touched her like that. ''Jake.''

''You were right,'' he said thickly. ''You deserve to be loved by the man who becomes your husband. Christine, I want to be that man.''

''Good.'' She wrapped her arms around his neck and lowered his head to hers. She had her proposal and his love. ''Because you're the man I pick.''

Epilogue

Christine stepped into the waiting room and grinned at the small group seated on the chairs. Jake held Anna on his lap while Jessie was comfortably settled on Rebecca's. They all turned expectant faces toward her when she opened the door.

"A beautiful baby boy," she announced. "Seven pounds, nine ounces, nineteen inches long. And a voice even louder than yours," she told Jessie with a smile.

Jessie jumped off her great-grandmother's lap and grabbed Christine's hand. "When can I see him? When can I see him?"

Christine met Jake's amused glance over the little girl's head. She ran her free hand over the shiny hair. "As soon as he's cleaned up and your mother's ready. Your dad said he would come get you."

"How did the doctor do?"

Christine grinned at Rebecca. "As well as could be expected. He was very controlled and giving demands as usual until . . ." Her lips curved upward at the memory of how quickly Dr. Greg Sanders had reverted to his role of husband when Mandy began shouting at him to get things finished. "Let's just say, he didn't need his white coat most of the time."

Jake and Rebecca laughed. "I'll be back as soon as I can," she promised them. "I wanted to give you the news right away."

She peeked into the recovery room. Greg sat next to Mandy's bed, his arm encircling his wife and child. The baby was cradled against Mandy's shoulder. Both heads were bowed toward the infant, identical expressions of awe on their faces.

Christine backed away from the door, a shimmer of tears in her eyes. Barely conscious of the gesture, she rested her hands at her waist and then went down the hall to finish the paperwork that would signal the arrival of David Michael Sanders into the world.

"So," Jake whispered against her ear as they stood outside the nursery window a half an hour later, "did you get any ideas?"

He held her firmly against his side. They had spent some time with the new mother before Jessie dragged them down the hall to show off her new brother. She was proudly explaining to Anna that he had all of his toes and fingers. "Mom showed me when I held him," she said with a lofty air.

"When we have a baby," Anna declared, "I'll get to hold him and even give him a bath." She glanced at Christine quickly, relaxing when she received an affirmative nod.

Christine rested her hand on her stomach and turned back to Jake. "What kind of ideas?" she asked carefully.

Jake kissed the top of her head. "A family. Babies. I know we haven't been married that long, but since we already have the start of a family . . .'' He lifted a hand toward Anna and shrugged. ''Why wait?''

''Well, I was thinking that Thanksgiving might be a good time.''

He rubbed his chin. ''Thanksgiving. That means the baby would come when?'' He paused and she could almost see him doing the math. ''Next summer.'' He gave another shrug. ''That would be fine. If that's what you want.''

''Actually . . .'' She chewed on her lower lip. ''Actually, I was thinking more in the line of having a baby by Thanksgiving.''

He frowned, the calculations apparent on his face again. ''I may not be the medically trained one here, but that doesn't leave us enough time, does it?''

She framed his face with her hands and kissed him on the lips. ''For an organized businessman, Jake Reynolds, you can be rather dense sometimes.'' She captured his hands with hers and rested them on her stomach just above the waistline. ''We've already started that extended family you're interested in.''

''What?'' He stared at her a moment and then at their joined hands before letting out a whoop. He grabbed her around the waist and spun her around before quickly dropping her back to the ground.

''I'm sorry, you're okay, right, that didn't cause any problems did it?''

She grinned at the worry in his eyes and smoothed a hand over his cheek. ''I'm fine. In fact, I couldn't be better.''

''A baby.'' He glanced through the window separating them from the nursery and then back at Christine.

At the soft look in his eyes, her knees threatened to give way. His arms wrapped around her, bringing her close. The kiss was sweet and full of promise, a vow that he would be there, that they would share in the care of this child just as they shared in the care of Anna.

"I love you," he whispered against her lips. He leaned his forehead against hers. "You don't mind if I announce this to everybody, do you?"

She shook her head. A tug of excitement and adventure rushed through her, wiping away the last dregs of restlessness, as she listened to the ring of pride in his voice as he made the announcement and received the congratulations of their friends.

Jake kept her securely anchored to his side and she rested her head on his shoulder. This was the man she loved, the father of her children. Snug within his arms, she knew she was where she belonged.